Game, Set, Murder

A Madeline Quinn Mystery, Book 1

Monique L. Stover

Laughing Buddha Press

Sign up for Monique L. Stover's newsletter at:
www.MoniqueLStover.com

*In loving memory of my mom, who introduced me to cozy mysteries.
And for my dad, who has always believed in me and continues to encourage my dreams.*

GAME, SET, MURDER

MONIQUE L. STOVER

Chapter One

Friday, September 26

The last thing I expected today was to find a body.

You would think that in a cozy little town like Sycamore Cove, you'd have no murders at all, but unfortunately people are just people. And it's my opinion that everyone is capable of murder, if given the right circumstances.

It all started with the annual tennis tournament.

Sycamore Cove, California, my home town, is so named for its abundance of sycamore trees and proximity to the ocean. It sits nestled in a valley surrounded by low mountain ranges on the north, east, and west sides, and to the south is the glorious Pacific Ocean. Just off the coast, you can see two small islands. Thanks to the mountains and nearby water, the climate here is Mediterranean, with moderate temperatures for most of the year.

With just under ten thousand people, you get to see a lot of the same people every day, but it's large enough to not feel cramped. We have relatively affordable townhouses near the ocean (which is where I live) and more expensive waterfront homes on Whale Watch Harbor. We also have a lot of agricultural land, which keeps the air smelling clean. Well, when they're not fertilizing or harvesting broccoli, that is. There are lemon groves, orange orchards, and avocado trees. The flowers of citrus trees smell just divine!

As we were now in September, I'd started seeing pumpkin patches popping up here and there. Three families calling themselves Conejo Family Farms even have hay rides and a petting zoo at their pumpkin patch!

I've lived here all of my life, so I know most of Sycamore Cove's small business owners. I am also one myself! I own a tennis shop called "Lucky Clover Tennis Shop." It's located on Ventura Boulevard (which is our town's main street), and is named after my beautiful Tuxedo cat, "Lucky Clover" - or just "Clover" for short. When my maternal grandparents passed away and left me some money in their will, I knew immediately that's what I wanted to do with it.

Speaking of tennis, today was one of my favorite times of the year outside of our Fall Festival.

The yearly tennis tournament!

This was a women's league tournament. So today we were competing to play in the Nationals. Our league was the Ventura County, California league.

Players who won their local leagues would first advance to district and sectional championships, then the winners of those sectional tournaments would represent their section at the USTA League National Championships.

The tennis tournament also happened to be one of our town's favorite events, so anyone who could get away from their daily responsibilities was here. It was a veritable who's who of Sycamore Cove.

The tournament was held at the largest tennis club in town, the Sycamore Cove Tennis Club. The club's sprawling property included eight tennis courts and an eighteen-hole golf course. It also had a fantastic restaurant.

Those of us waiting to play in the tournament sat or stood around a unique tennis court that felt a bit like being in a colosseum. The floor of the court was below ground level and was surrounded on all sides by large, grass-covered steps which doubled as spectator seats. My best friend Lizzy Mitchell and I were sitting on one of these large steps.

Lizzy is my age. Twenty-five. We've been best friends since kindergarten, but you'd be hard-pressed to find two people less alike. Lizzy is five feet short and is a gorgeous, curvy half-Samoan woman with cafe-latte skin and long, wavy dark hair. She owned the town's only candle bar and gift shop, Wicked Wicks.

I, on the other hand, am a five-foot, seven-inch skinny Irish girl, with pale skin, green eyes, and long, cherry-red hair (which was usually up in a ponytail).

Oh, and my name is Madeline Quinn. Mads for short, though family still calls me Maddie.

As we waited for the tournament to begin, my younger brother Rick passed by. He's nearly six feet tall and is super buff. But he is also three years younger than I am, so he'll always be my little brother. Like me, the poor kid was stuck with the same red hair and pale complexion.

He stopped on a lower step where he could look us in the eye.

"Hey, Sis!" Rick said. He turned to Lizzy with a big smile. "Hey Liz."

He sat there staring at her for a minute. Finally, I cleared my throat and he turned back to me.

"So, Rick," I said. "Please get some really cool shots of me playing today. Oh, and of Lizzy too, of course." Rick is a full-time, freelance photographer. Today's photos would end up in our local newspaper, the Ventura County Star.

"Of course!" he said agreeably. "Bye Sis! Bye Liz!" With a wave, he headed off into the crowd.

The club had installed some temporary seating and umbrellas for the spectators. I could see my parents (Camille and Bobby), and Pops (my grandfather), all sitting close to the front row. Even my older sister Annabelle made it! At only thirty-two years old, she was appointed Chief of Police. This made her the first woman, and the youngest person, to hold the role in our town. It's pretty impressive, when even the Chief of Police makes time for the tournament. Next to Annabelle sat her husband, Sean. Sean is a fireman. This worked out well with Annabelle's job as he was often able to be at home with my niece, Summer, when my sister was busy with work.

Lizzy and I waved madly at them, getting big smiles and waves in return. Summer in particular jumped up and down with a level of excitement only a five-year-old could manage.

"Look, Lizzy!" I said, having spotted Clover's veterinarian. "It's Vicki Schmidt! Rats. I keep forgetting to make Clover's yearly checkup appointment."

As if Vicki were reading my mind, she waved then pointed at her watch. I nodded in acknowledgement. "Yeah, yeah," I muttered.

As the wait for the tournament started to drag on, I looked longingly at Kay's Koffee Kart. Kay Bowman had the cutest little coffee shop right in the harbor. I would go there almost every week just to grab a coffee and pastry. I'd sit outside and watch the yachts glide regally through the harbor canals on their way out to the ocean.

Lizzy nudged me. "Mads! It's time!" She wiggled with excitement. Not just for the tennis, but also because her parents, Dan and Emma, were the ones kicking things off.

Dan Mitchell was a handsome man in his late fifties. His short hair was just turning gray at the edges and sideburns. A closely trimmed salt and pepper goatee made him look quite distinguished. As the director of the tennis club, he spent a lot of time outside overseeing the tennis program, lessons, and tournaments, so he was tan, and as an ex-tennis-pro, he was also fit. His wife Emma was the mayor of Sycamore Cove. Emma, a few years younger, was one hundred percent Samoan and was stunning, just like Lizzy.

Dan stood by the microphone and made a silent request for quiet, by raising his hands to the crowd. Eager for the games to start, everyone complied immediately.

Dan leaned toward the mic. "Welcome! Welcome, every-one! Emma and I are so glad to see that so many residents of our little town could make it to today's tournament!"

At this, a cheer rose from the crowd. Dan and Emma laughed appreciatively and waited for quiet to return. When it did, Emma took the mic from her husband.

"Hello. I'm your mayor." A chuckle went through the crowd, as everyone there was quite familiar with her. "I'd like to give a big 'thank you' to Kay's Koffee for providing the caffeine and snacks for today's matches. And to Patty's Party Palace for the seating and umbrellas, and to our very own tennis champion, Madeline Quinn of the Lucky Clover Tennis Shop, for today's tennis balls." A cheer went up from the stands. I waved at the crowd in appreciation. When things quieted down again, Emma continued.

"Players: when we're done here, you will meet with your coaches and then head to the tables with the blue tablecloths to see who you will be matched with. After the tournament, please join us at Pop's Pizza for a celebration. No matter who wins the matches, you're all winners to me. Let the games begin!"

Yes, Pops, aka Edward Quinn, was my grandfather on my dad's side, and owned the local pizza place. Boy was that fun growing up! I think I had friends that I never would have otherwise made thanks to free pizza at Pop's.

~

WHILE LIZZY'S PARENTS TOOK THEIR SEATS IN THE FRONT ROW of the stands, Lizzy and I made our way to the tables to see who we'd be matched against.

My knee ached from an old injury dating back to my junior tennis days, but I ignored it. I was so nervous, I could hardly focus. After looking at the draw for the day, it unfortunately looked like I might end up playing against a left-handed player named Tracy, if she won the right matches. She was not only good, but watching her play left-handed gave her a definite advantage over me. I found her facing the "wrong" way very disorienting. Thankfully, as we turned back toward the tennis courts, I was soon distracted by a pleasant surprise.

My tennis coach, Matteo Amato, was making his way toward me. That got me more than a few glances of envy and even jealousy from some of the other players, as he was a tall, dark, and hunky Italian-American.

I'll admit, my chest puffed up with just a little bit of pride at the attention.

He gave me a warm smile of encouragement. "You're going to do just great today, Mads. You just have to relax and enjoy yourself. Enjoy the game of tennis. It's the best in the world."

"Thanks, Coach!" I impulsively gave him a hug of appreciation. To my surprise, I heard a grunt of what sounded like pain. I quickly let go and backed away. "Oh! Are you okay? Did I hurt you?"

I thought how silly that question must have sounded to him. I may be on the tall side, but how could a woman like me hurt a guy like that?

His right arm wrapped around his rib cage, and he winced in pain. "No, you're good. I think I may have bruised a rib. Probably during weights this morning."

Next thing I knew, Sharon Christensen was standing next to me. Sharon was one of the tournament players and also the mother of a player, Denise. Sharon was attractive, with short blonde hair, and looked younger than she was. I knew her daughter Denise was twenty-four, so I guessed Sharon to be in her early forties.

"What did you do to him Mads?" Sharon asked. "Did you step on his foot or something? He's obviously in pain." Sharon winked at Coach Matteo, pretending to look him up and down critically in an apparent search for damage.

At this, Coach Matteo made an effort to drop his arm and give me another smile, albeit a bit tighter than the last. "All good, Sharon. Just some rib pain. Break a leg, Mads!" He started to turn away, then turned back with a quick, "You too, Sharon." He left us to give a few other players some words of encouragement. He really was a great coach.

"Hmm. Well, that was odd," Sharon said with a frown.

I heard my number called over the PA system. It was my turn on the court!

"Sorry Sharon! I have to go. I'm up!" I gave my ponytail a quick tightening, grabbed my racket, and stepped onto the deuce side of the court to serve the ball. It was my serve first, and I was glad of it.

I have a killer serve.

I tossed the ball, high and slow. Time seemed to stop, and my eye caught a glimpse of white, puffy clouds in a cerulean blue sky. Then THWACK! I smashed the ball into the white box on the other side of the net. The game was on.

Playing tennis always took one hundred percent of my attention and gave me great joy. So in what seemed like no time at all, the match was over, and I had won it. Grinning and sweaty I jogged off the court to stand next to Lizzy.

"Woot!" she said quietly, so as not to distract the new set

of players that had taken the court. "Great playing, Mads! You're still as amazing as ever!"

I shrugged off the compliment with a shy smile. "Well, I don't know about that. I just got lucky that I wasn't paired with Tracy. Who knew that being left-handed could be such an advantage?"

Lizzy looked at me sideways with a smirk. "Yeah, that would have been an unlucky event. And my girl Madeline isn't unlucky."

I gave her a wink, and we sat to watch the rest of the tournament together.

◆

THE TOURNAMENT WAS STILL GOING STRONG, WHEN AN HOUR or so later, my eye caught a disruption just outside the tennis court boundaries, almost at the parking lot. I elbowed Lizzie and said, "Hey! What do you think is going on over there?"

A man with a picket sign that said, "Pickleballers deserve courts too!" started yelling loudly over the noise of the match. "Pickleballers have rights too! We deserve to have our own courts!" He paced back and forth, shaking his sign in vigorous anger.

The heads of the tournament spectators all turned in his direction. And so did the heads of the two coaches, Coach Matteo and Coach Masayuki.

Coach Matteo strode quickly toward the pickleball guy. When the picketer noticed a wall of lithe muscle coming toward him with a scowl on his face, he lowered his sign and started to run toward the parking lot, and presumably his car.

They started to struggle, then both men were out of sight.

Lizzie and I looked at each other. "Did you see that?" we both asked at the same time.

"I wish we could leave the tournament to go over there and see what's going on!" I said to Lizzy.

"We can't leave! You have another match soon. We'll ask Coach Matteo about it when we see him at the pizza party," Lizzy said. "I think I know who he's arguing with."

Reluctantly, I nodded in agreement.

When the tournament ended, Lizzy and I took some time to accept congratulations from our families and fellow players on winning our matches. Lizzy had won two out of three matches, and I had won in straight sets. We'd be moving on to part two of the tournament the following week. It was time to celebrate!

But first, I grabbed my tennis bag and said, "Come on, Lizzy. Let's go see if we can find Coach Matteo. I'm worried about him and that pickleball guy." I grabbed her hand and dragged her behind me, heading toward the locker rooms next to the parking lot.

"Okay, okay! I'm coming. You don't have to tear my arm off," Lizzy said.

I looked back at her sheepishly. "Sorry!" I said, letting go of her arm.

Soon we felt like salmon swimming upstream when we encountered a small swarm of women heading away from the locker rooms and toward the parking lot - and us.

"Excuse me-, sorry-, pardon-, Augh!" Getting buffeted from all sides, I started to seriously consider using my racket or throwing some elbows. "Has anyone seen Coach Matteo?" I had to raise my voice to be heard over the constant thrumming and chattering of a gaggle of women. Thankfully I'd had drama in high school, so my voice carried.

And there was Sharon again! She was passing close by

and stopped, waving a hand at me. Her daughter, Denise, had to stop short to keep from barreling over her mom. "Oof!" she said.

Sharon took me by the elbow and led us away from the restrooms. Now it was my turn to get my arm pulled off. "Yes!" Sharon said. "We saw him leave shortly after the tournament was over, didn't we sweetheart?" She turned to her daughter who was now walking beside us, no doubt to avoid another near-collision.

"Um, sure. Yeah," Denise said.

I did a double-take. Did I just see Denise blush? I must be seeing things.

Sharon had started moving again, and had linked arms with me on one side and Lizzy on the other like something out of the Wizard of Oz.

"Ow!" Lizzy said. "What's the hurry"?

We still had our tennis gear with us, which was making it awkward, with all the bouncing of bags against our backs and hips.

"A party, that's what's the hurry!" Sharon said with a smile. "We won the tournament! Coach Matteo and Coach Masayuki are throwing a party for us at Pop's Pizza. I'm sure that's where they are, setting things up."

I nodded. "Oh, yeah. Maybe that's where he is then."

Finally at the parking lot, Sharon let us go. Sharon's husband, Steve, was waiting by their Maserati SUV with the hatchback open, ready to relieve them of their tennis gear.

"Hi, Steve!" I said with a wave. He gave me a short nod, grunt, and semi-smile. I heard him ask Sharon, "Where is Denise's bag?"

Lizzy and I turned toward my car. "I'm sure he's just tired from a day in the sun," I muttered to Lizzy under my breath. "Right?"

We gave each other a look. "Yeah, right," Lizzy said.

As the Christensens packed up their car, Lizzy and I headed toward mine.

It may not be a Maserati, but I love my car. It's a custom, shamrock-green, convertible Fiat. Maybe it's an impractical car, but hey, I'm a single, twenty-five-year-old woman with a cat, not a soccer mom with five kids. On each of the doors, I have a cute little magnetic sign advertising my business, the "Lucky Clover Tennis Shop." You can't say my car isn't eye-catching!

Lizzy and I dumped our gear into the back seat, opened up the convertible top, and headed toward my house for some much-needed showers. There was no way I was going to a celebration smelling like a locker room. Even if it was my own grandfather's pizza place. Besides, I was hoping to spend some time with Coach Matteo. Is it bad to have a crush on your tennis coach?

Anyway, I lived in an adorable little community of townhomes close to the beach. There were approximately twenty buildings, each with three townhomes: two end units and a unit sandwiched in between. Each townhome was three stories. The bottom floor had a garage at the back and a nice little patio at the front. The second floor held the kitchen, living room, and a balcony. The third floor had two bedrooms, each with their own en suite bathroom and a balcony off the primary bedroom. The unit I had purchased was in the row of buildings closest to the ocean. I had an end unit and my balconies faced the ocean. It was the first thing I bought when my tennis shop became reliably successful, and I absolutely adored it!

A few minutes later, we pulled up to my townhome and parked in the garage. We went upstairs to the kitchen and living room area and dumped our gear bags onto the floor.

I lifted my chin toward Lizzy. "You shower first. I need to feed Clover." As if on cue, Clover, my beautiful Tuxedo cat, sauntered up, giving each of us a good leg rub and shoe sniff.

"Meow," Clover said.

"Yes," I replied. "Meow, indeed! We won, Clover!" At that, she flopped onto her side and stretched into a crescent moon shape. "Ooh, yes. Did you miss me? Because I missed you!" I gave her exposed belly a gentle rub with both hands, getting a nice little purr in response.

As I rubbed Clover's belly, I thought about tonight's celebration. While it's always nice to celebrate a win in tennis, I was especially eager to find Coach Matteo and ask about how things went with the pickleball guy.

Seeing me thinking hard, Clover stood up and gave me another rub across the legs. I could hear her purring, so I picked her up for some quick kitty cuddles. Nothing made me feel better than kitty cuddles! She purred some more as I nuzzled my face into her soft fur. Somehow cats always smelled so good.

"I love you, my little Lucky Clover! Be good and I'll see you after the pizza party." With one last kiss, I set her back down.

Leaving her grooming on the floor, I opened up a can of wet cat food and put it into a clean bowl. I topped off her water and guzzled a bottle of water myself.

Lizzy came down the stairs smelling fresh and clean, and wearing a cute outfit she'd brought to change into for the party. We were going to party whether we won the tournament or not.

"Your turn!" she said, putting her dirty tennis clothes into my washing machine, which was hidden from sight behind two fake-shutter doors.

"Yes," I said, giving her a sideways glance. "I'd be happy to wash your smelly tennis clothes for you."

She had the good sense to look a little guilty. "Thank you. You know what my apartment's laundry room is like! I'd hate for their crappy old machines to eat my only tennis outfit. Those things are pricey! Even with the friends & family discount." She smiled at me.

"Agreed," I said. "Don't worry about it. Back in a flash!" With that, I ran upstairs for a shower.

~

BY THE TIME LIZZY AND I ARRIVED AT THE PIZZA PLACE, THE party was already hopping.

"Come on! There's an open spot at that table!" Lizzy said, pointing to a table that already held the Christensen family and a few others. Mads's parents could be seen helping Pops with the crowd.

We sat down with hellos and dug right into the open boxes of pizzas and pitchers of sodas and beers. Tennis always made me feel super healthy afterwards, so I opted for the veggie toppings and some iced water rather than my usual "meat lovers" pizza and full-sugar Coca Cola.

We were all talking and laughing when Coach Masayuki came up to our table. He was a lanky Japanese American, who had a kind face and was soft-spoken, when not yelling at students. He was accompanied by a pretty, young, brunette woman. Or girl, really. She couldn't have been much over sixteen.

"Hello, folks!" Coach Masayuki said. "I'd like for you to meet Courtney Engelmann. She is a tennis phenom that I'm fortunate enough to coach. She's gonna be a big star soon. You mark my words." He smiled at her like he had spawned her himself.

"Nice to meet you all," she said shyly. "Hi, Denise," she added with a small smile. "Good playing today."

"Thanks Court," Denise replied.

"Would you two like to join us?" I asked.

"Oh, no. Gotta keep making the rounds with Courtney here," Coach Masayuki said. With that, they were on their way to another table.

After they were out of earshot, Sharon leaned over conspiratorially and said in a stage whisper, "Yeah. That big star is going to make him some big money someday."

"Mom!" Denise flushed with embarrassment.

"What? I'm just saying what everyone else is thinking."

"Sharon! That's inappropriate," her husband Steve said with a frown.

"What?" Sharon shrugged and took a long draw of her beer. "Just saying."

"I thought Court was Coach Matteo's student," Denise said, looking around the table. She was met with blank stares and shrugs.

"I heard Coach Masayuki stole Courtney from Coach Matteo," Sharon said.

We all looked at her in shock.

"What?" I said. "Why would he do that?" I couldn't believe what I was hearing.

Sharon just shrugged.

Trying to change the subject, I asked, "Speaking of Coach Matteo, does anyone know where he is?" I stood up to look around the room. Despite my height, as we had taken up more than half of the place, it was hard to pick out a particular person even for me.

I turned to Lizzy and the others and said, "Be right back."

I started to move around the room looking for, and asking about, Coach Matteo. Mostly I got some blank stares, shrugs, or head shakes.

"Have you seen Denise Christensen? He's probably with *her*," one woman said with a roll of her eyes.

Another woman gave a short laugh and said, "Oh, I don't know. Go find the prettiest girl here that's over twenty. He's likely to be found there."

After a few of these types of comments, I just stopped and frowned in confusion and surprise. Coach Matteo was a womanizer? How did I never see this?

I went to find Lizzy and pulled her away from our table into a semi-private corner. I told her about the responses I'd gotten from more than a few people, men and women alike.

"How did I not know this about him?" I asked in dismay. I really looked up to and admired Coach Matteo. This really hurt.

"Wow," Lizzy said. "I never imagined. Though I suppose a true player knows how to make all of his paramours feel special."

We both shook our heads in disbelief.

"Well, he's not here, so far as I can tell," I said. "I guess we should just rejoin the party for a bit then call it a night."

Lizzy nodded in agreement. "Yeah, this has kinda taken all of the fun out of it."

We went back to our table and half-heartedly picked at our food.

"You girls alright?" Sharon asked after a while. "You've gotten awfully quiet."

Not wanting her to know that her daughter may have been a target of Coach Matteo's broad affections, I just said, "Yeah. I think we're just beat. It kinda came on suddenly."

"Did you ever find Matteo? I mean, Coach Matteo?" Denise asked, looking around hopefully.

Sharon looked at her daughter sharply, eyes narrowed.

I turned toward Sharon in shock. Was she... *jealous?*

~

As the party wound down, I pulled Lizzy aside.

"Hey Lizzy," I said. "Can you let my family know I left and maybe catch a ride home with them? I am worried about Coach Matteo. I tried calling him, but he didn't answer. I want to head back to the tennis club to see if he's still there."

Lizzy looked at me with concern. "Do you want me to go with you? It's late. I don't want you to be alone."

"Don't be silly," I said more bravely than I felt. "I practically grew up at that place. I'm sure there will still be some folks there finishing cleaning up from the tournament today."

"If you say so," Lizzy said. "Call if you need me for anything, okay?"

We gave each other a hug goodbye, and I headed out to my car.

When I arrived at the club, I spotted Coach Matteo's car and parked next to it. So he *was* still here! With a sigh of relief, I jogged toward the courts. The sun had long since gone down, but the courts and club grounds were well lit. Maybe he was working with some students that didn't fare as well in their matches.

However, he was not on any of the courts. I stopped one of the men folding up the spectator seats and asked, "Have you seen Coach Matteo since the tournament?" He shook his head no, so I continued my search. When I didn't see him in the little gift shop, or near the pool, I pulled out my phone and started to walk past the women's locker room and restroom toward the men's, which was a bit farther down. As I walked, I dialed Coach's number.

Ah! He was still in the men's locker room. I could hear his ringtone from where I was standing.

"Coach? You in there?" I asked. The tennis club's restrooms and locker rooms were laid out so that when you first enter, you see a line of ceramic sinks with one long mirror on the wall. To the one side of the sinks, were the bathroom stalls. To the other, were rows and rows of tall metal lockers, and beyond that, showers.

I walked into the men's bathroom sink area as far as I dared. I didn't want to catch him unaware. Not that I'd mind catching him without a shirt-

I stopped dead in my tracks. There, on the floor under one of the ceramic sinks, was Coach Matteo.

My breath caught as tears filled my eyes. I began to shake, and my chest clenched in grief and shock.

"Oh, God, no," I said.

Slowly, I walked closer to him.

I didn't need to check for a pulse. He was obviously dead, his head at an odd angle. The blood was another clue. It was all over the sink, floor, and mirrored wall.

Hands shaking, I dialed 911. I barely heard, but I think they said help was on the way.

They had asked me to wait outside, away from the body. But I was drawn to the odd-looking marks on his body. It looked familiar, for some reason. There seemed to be some kind of pattern to them - almost like an SOS in Morse code. Long dash. Space. Long dash. Hmm.

Before I realized what I was doing, I had taken a few photos of the body and the crime scene. There were spatterings of blood on the mirrors and wall in long streaks which thinned out the closer they got to the ceiling. It looked almost as though someone was replicating a Jackson Pollock painting. On the floor, even to my untrained eye, I could see that there were shoe marks in and around the blood pools that were there. I also noticed that he was still wearing the same tennis outfit he had on earlier today.

My heart broke for the coach.

When I heard the emergency vehicles arrive, I quickly

moved out into the hallway. I went out to meet them so I could lead them to poor Coach Matteo's body.

I was met by a uniformed policeman accompanied by someone I assumed to be a detective.

~

THE GRIM-LOOKING POLICE OFFICER GUARDED THE DOOR TO the locker room, while the detective stopped to speak with me.

"My name is Detective Doug Dougan. You're the one who found the body?" he asked. Detective Dougan looked a bit like you might expect. He had on a nice, but wrinkled dark suit. His tie was a somber brown as were his patent leather, laced shoes. He looked like he was on his tenth cup of coffee. He must have been new to Sycamore Cove, as I did not recognize him.

"Yes, sir," I said, still wiping tears from my eyes. "I found the body."

"Your name?"

"Madeline Quinn."

"Quinn, hmm?" His mouth twitched, but he didn't give any other indication that he suspected I was his Chief's sister. The detective jotted some notes onto a small notepad, then looked back up at me. "You knew the victim?"

"Yes," I said. "He is, uh, was, my tennis coach."

"I'm sorry for your loss," he said. I nodded my thanks. "How did you come to find the body?"

"We had a tennis tournament today. When he didn't show up at the pizza party afterwards, I thought I should come back to the club to look for him."

"You didn't think he just went home instead of to the party?" Dougan asked.

"Oh, no. He never misses our tennis parties," I said, shaking my head.

"Did you touch anything in the room? The body?"

"No, sir," I said. Which was true. But I wasn't going to volunteer that I had taken photos.

Detective Dougan nodded. "Do you know of anyone who might have wanted to harm him?"

I started to cry again. "No," I said through my tears. "He was a really great guy! Though he did get into an argument with a pickleball protester at today's tournament." I pulled a tissue out of my purse and wiped my nose. "I only saw the argument from the other side of the courts, but it didn't look pleasant."

The detective nodded again, folded his notebook, and put it in his suit pocket. "I'm going to need you to come down to the station to make a formal statement," he said. With a look at his watch, he added, "It's already pretty late. Why don't we do that in the morning. I'll be working all weekend anyway."

"Okay. Thank you, Detective."

Turning away from me, Detective Dougan tapped the officer on the shoulder, and they entered the crime scene together. I noticed that they stepped very carefully so as not to disturb any possible evidence.

Curious, I moved back into the shadows of the walkway to watch them do their job. The detective crouched near the body and made a few more notes, then stood up again. He said something to the officer that I couldn't hear, who then said something into his radio.

After a few minutes, two people with "Forensic Services Bureau" on their jackets placed little booties over their shoes, then entered the locker room.

To my complete surprise, I recognized one of the crime scene technicians from high school! Not just anyone, but my high school crush, Jeremy Miller. Jeremy? A field evidence technician? And wow... he had filled out nicely. He was two years older than me, so I was still only a sophomore when he graduated, but I had two whole years to pine away for him. And although he was on the football team, and was pretty popular, he never ignored me. He'd say hello in the hallways or hold the door for me now and then. And now there he was.

I immediately chided myself for these thoughts while poor Coach Matteo lay dead on the floor. What was wrong with me?

I watched the crime scene investigators, or CSIs, as they carefully placed paper bags over the Coach's hands. I wondered if they thought perhaps he had scratched his killer.

There appeared to be shoe prints both in the blood pools as well as blood-red prints on the tile where the killer probably stepped after stepping in the blood. Depending on what Jeremy was collecting, he used various chemicals, sheets of thin plastic, and took lots of photos.

He then pulled what appeared to be two or three long hairs from the blood using tweezers. The other CSI spent most of her time photographing and tracking the potential paths of the blood on the mirror and wall using strings that stretched from the body to various spots on the wall.

I was enraptured by the whole process.

Finally, Jeremy, who had been bent over the body, stood up and said, "We're ready for the medical examiner." His deep voice carried across the locker room to my ears. My tummy fluttered at the sound.

The detective left the locker room, followed by the two technicians. The officer stayed behind to wait for the Medical Examiner.

When Jeremy passed close by me, I quietly cleared my throat to get his attention. He stopped in surprise and turned toward my spot in the shadows. I stepped forward a bit so he could see me.

"Who..." Jeremy began. Then his eyes widened as he recognized me. "Madeline Quinn? Maddie, is that you?"

"Hi Jeremy," I said.

"Oh wow!" he said, then frowned in concern. "What are you doing here?"

"I found the body," I said. Dang it! I started to tear up again! Like my nose wasn't already red enough?

"Oh, my God," Jeremy said. "I'm so sorry, Maddie. That's terrible." He looked like he wanted to hug me, but his arms were filled with evidence bags and his field kit.

But I loved him anew for that impulse.

"You coming in to make a statement?" he asked.

"Yes," I said. "The detective said I could do it tomorrow morning."

Jeremy nodded in agreement. "Good plan."

We stared at each other for a few moments, until someone yelled Jeremy's name from somewhere near the courts. "Jer! Get a move on! We don't have all night!"

He winced. "Sorry. Gotta go." He started to walk away, then stopped and turned back to me. "See you tomorrow?"

"Count on it," I said with a smile.

On the way to my car, I was saddened again by the sight of Coach Matteo's car being towed away.

Chapter Two

Saturday, September 27

Saturday morning, I mentally prepared myself for giving an official statement to Detective Dougan at the station. Despite having found a body in eleventh grade, I never had to go in and speak to a detective. Likely because of my age at the time. It was early in the school year, so I was still only seventeen. My parents were there and it was an easy guess to figure out that I wasn't a suspect in the murder of the high school janitor. It was the first time I'd ever seen a dead body. Still, I was as surprised as everyone else when the evidence I'd discovered turned out to be key to solving the case. They even wrote an article about me in the school paper and the town paper. That case made my sister's career. It eventually led to her being promoted to Chief.

This time, I was not only an adult, but I knew the victim much more personally.

Detective Dougan let me sit alone for almost an hour before he came into the interrogation room. Good thing I hadn't had any liquids in a while. If he thought I'd be begging for the bathroom, he'd better think again. Yes, despite this being a statement, I was in an interrogation room. This made me think that maybe he didn't like me very much.

He finally came into the room looking down at a folder filled with papers in his hand, not making eye contact with me at all. He leaned against a desk that was in the corner and crossed his legs at the ankles. He continued to read for a few minutes before looking up. Points number two and three that he didn't like me. Or maybe he just wanted to throw me off. Keep me on my toes.

I waited patiently. Between two siblings and a tendency to get bullied in school when I was younger, I wasn't easily intimidated.

"Let's get started, shall we Miss..." He looked at his folder as though he couldn't remember my last name. Then said, "Miss Quinn." He looked back up.

"Sure. Where would you like for me to start?"

"How about at the beginning?"

I told him about arriving at the club after the pizza party, then going to look for Coach Matteo in the locker room area.

"So you followed his ringing phone," Detective Dougan said.

"Yes."

"Did you touch or move the body?"

"No."

"You sure? You didn't, for example, check him for a pulse?"

"No."

"Why not?" he asked.

Well, that sounded more accusatory than I liked. I narrowed my eyes at him. "It was more than obvious that he was dead."

"Oh, so you're a doctor now?" he asked.

"I'm not going to dignify that with a response. I found his

body. I didn't touch anything. I called you. End of story." I crossed my arms across my chest and went silent.

Detective Dougan nodded slowly. Then he surprised me with an unexpected question.

"It's my understanding," he said, "that this is not the first time you've found a body."

My jaw dropped. I thought those records were sealed due to my age.

His eyebrows raised in question.

"Um, yes. I did. In high school," I said slowly. I needed time to think. But I guess if he knew about it, there wasn't much to be done at this point except be honest. I just really hated talking about it. It was not a pleasant experience.

"I was a junior, so I was seventeen," I said. "I found the body of our high school's janitor in the boiler room. The janitor of our school was a really great guy. He watched over us kids like we were his own. Unfortunately, there was a boy, a senior, who was a troublemaker. The janitor called him out on something he did, and the boy's dad killed the janitor to protect his son's future as a lawyer, or some such nonsense. I found one of the father's custom-made cuff links that had slid out of sight in the boiler room. This was enough to get the dad convicted." I looked down at my hands and picked at a nail. Just thinking about it made me sad again. The janitor was such a nice man.

The detective said quietly, "I'm sorry you had to deal with that at such young age."

I looked up in surprise. "Uh, thank you."

"Thank you for coming in, Miss Quinn. Have a nice day." At that, he got up and left. On his way out, he held the door open for my sister who was coming in as he left.

"Detective," she said to him with a nod.

"Chief," he replied.

Now that it was over, the emotions started to hit. I felt my eyes tear up. "I lose a friend and this is how I'm treated? At your own department?" I'll admit, I was channeling my fear and emotions toward her. Right or wrong, anger felt better. Like I was more in control.

She sighed. "That's just it, Maddie. It's my department. I couldn't let anyone think you were getting special treatment because you're the Chief's sister. You understand that, right?" she asked.

Damn it. I hate it when she's right.

"If you don't have to be at the tennis shop today," she said kindly, "you may want to go home and get some rest."

My anger fizzled, and I was now more sad than anything else. "Yeah, that's a good idea." I stood up and we gave each other a hug.

"Love you, Sis," I said into her hair.

"Love you back," she said.

Once in the hallway, she went off toward her office and I turned toward the front desk to see myself out. That's when I spotted Jeremy. The sight of him pulled me like a magnet.

"Jeremy!" I called out as I ran toward him. I slammed up against him and wrapped my arms around him. To my utter embarrassment, I started to cry. Again!

"Woah, there! Maddie! Are you okay?" he asked. He gently pushed me away so he could look me in the eyes.

"Yes, sorry to assault you like that," I said with an embarrassed smile.

Oh, my god. We barely knew each other and I just made a whole scene at his place of employment. I could feel eyes on me from nearby cubicles.

"I just gave my statement to Detective Dougan," I said, wiping my eyes on my sleeve.

Jeremy looked at me in shock. "Is he the one that made you this upset? For a simple statement?" He looked around for the detective with anger burning in his hazel green eyes.

His hands dropped to his side and he balled them into fists. "I'm gonna have a little conversation of my own with him."

"No, Jeremy, it's okay, really," I said, trying to diffuse his anger. I was touched that he cared so much, but I didn't want him getting into trouble over me, so I gathered myself together and said, "I'm all right now, really." I rallied a smile to seem more convincing.

Jeremy smiled back. "Okay, if you say so. But I can't promise I won't be having a conversation with Detective Dougan about this."

At that, Jeremy went back to work and I headed out to my car as quickly as I could, so as not to run into my sister or the detective again.

$\sim$

ON MY DRIVE HOME, I KEPT THINKING ABOUT WAYS I COULD have handled that better. I didn't really have anything to hide, but the detective put me on the defensive and that changed the whole tone of the conversation. I suppose he'd managed to get what he needed out of me, but he hadn't made a friend today.

I thought about the photos I'd taken. Had his approach with me been less confrontational, I likely would have told him about them, but I'm sure Jeremy or the other CSI had done their job and taken better photos than I ever could have.

But speaking of photos... in all the excitement I'd forgotten that my brother Rick had photos of the entire tournament!

I wanted to see those photos.

$\sim$

RICK AGREED TO COME BY MY HOUSE. WHEN HE ARRIVED, I had to run downstairs to let him in the front door.

"Hi Rick! Thanks for coming over," I said, giving my little brother a hug.

"No problem, Maddie. I have all of the photos I took at the tournament right here on my laptop." He held up his computer as though there could be any possible confusion as to there being some other laptop in question.

I ushered him up the stairs and into my living room.

"Have a seat. Can I get you anything?" I asked. "Coke? Water?" Rick set up his laptop on the coffee table while I raided my fridge.

"Ooh, yeah! A Coke sounds great. Got any chips and guac to go with that?"

I narrowed my eyes at him. "What am I, a restaurant?" Then my eyebrows shot up. "Wait! Yes, I do have some seed crackers and spreadable cheese." I showed him the items in question.

Rick turned and said, "Well, that sounds just a bit too healthy for my taste, but I'm in no position to argue. I'm famished!"

I gave him an exasperated look. "Well, if you're that hungry, I should just make you a sandwich."

"No arguments here, Sis! That would be swell, thanks!" He gave me a thumbs up and turned back to his computer.

"Gonna eat me out of house and home, he is," I mumbled to myself. "And who says 'swell' these days?" I said loud enough for him to hear me. It wasn't long before I had some sandwiches thrown together. Tuna for me, roast beef for him. I brought them and our drinks to the couch with me and set them on the coffee table.

By the time I had sat down with the food, Rick had the first of his photos cast to my big screen TV.

"So, what exactly are we looking for?" he asked, taking a

big bite of his sandwich. He made a yummy sound and closed his eyes in pleasure.

I won't lie. I felt a bit proud at this.

"I'm not sure yet, but I definitely want to see if there are any photos of the pickleball guy."

"Oh, there are," Rick said.

"Great. But let's go through them in order so we don't miss anything."

Rick nodded and began to page through photos of the warm ups. After a few minutes, we got to the start of the tournament and something caught my eye. My mouth was full, so I pointed with one hand (the other was holding my sandwich) and basically grunted my instructions to pause the show.

Rick stopped on a photo in which, behind the players in the foreground, I could see Coach Matteo and Coach Masayuki having an apparent argument. I asked Rick to look for any more photos he had of this argument. There were five different shots. All images of what appeared to be lots of yelling and pointing.

I set my sandwich down and turned to Rick. "Did you notice this fight as you were taking these photos?"

"No," Rick said with a shake of his head. "If I had, I would have zoomed in and taken more photos until the argument was over."

"Hmm," I said. "What do you think they're pointing at? Whatever it is, it might be the subject of their argument."

"Whatever? Or whoever? There are a lot of folks standing around, sitting in the stands, or playing tennis."

I stood up with a sudden idea.

"Meow!" Clover, who had just cuddled up next to me on the couch, got up as well, appearing offended at having been disturbed.

"Ooh, no! I'm sorry, baby!" I said. But she was having none

of it. She strode away, tail swishing at me as if shaking a finger.

"She'll be back," Rick assured me. "What are you thinking?"

I started to pace. Rick's head followed me as I moved around the room.

"At last night's pizza party, I remember Coach Masayuki introduced us to a new, young player. Someone that just might make him a lot of money one day, if Sharon is to be believed."

"Okay, so?"

"So... Denise said she thought Courtney was originally Coach Matteo's student, not Coach Masayuki's!" I turned to my brother with a triumphant look on my face. "Maybe *she* is *who* they were fighting about!"

"Despite the fact that I have no idea who any of these people are, that sounds like a plausible theory, Sis!"

"Okay. Let me replenish our drinks, then we can look at the rest of these photos," I said, heading into the kitchen.

We sat down with our fresh sodas and tediously went through several hundred more photos. We paused occasionally to comment on cute shots of Lizzy and me playing tennis, Mom and Dad cheering me on from the stands, and of my older sister, Annabelle.

Finally, we came to the photos I had in mind when I had first asked to see his shots.

The pickleball guy.

"There he is!" I yelled. Rick jumped and gave me a look. "Sorry. I got excited. That's the guy." I pointed at a man holding a sign. He was way over on the other side of the courts, so it was hard to make out, but by zooming in we got the gist of the conversation. It did not appear to be a pleasant one.

Who knew Coach Matteo had such an angry side to his personality?

As we looked through the photos featuring the pickleball man, we could see lots of gesturing and angry looks. Coach Matteo was grabbing the guy's sign and trying to wrest it away.

The pickleball guy wasn't having it. He was almost as tall as the coach, but quite a bit scrawny-er. Was that even a word? It was now.

"They're kinda blurry. Any chance you can sharpen them up somehow?" I asked.

"Not likely," Rick said. "I wasn't actually focused on the argument, so it wasn't in my depth of field. I was just lucky to catch some of the argument while I was focused on other people or objects."

"Drat," I said. "Well, at least the photos confirm what I thought I saw."

We went through the rest of the photos, but there was not much to see after the pickleball incident. Or as I now like to think of it: Picklegate. I'd have to spend time going through the photos again. It was a lot to take in all at once.

"Okay, Rick. This was amazing, thanks!" I said. "Can you send me a link or something to these so I can look at them some more when I have time? I have to get to the shop."

"I'll do ya one better," he said, as he packed up his stuff. "I made you a flash drive." He handed me a drive shaped like a cat. I cracked up.

"Look, Clover! A kitty cat flash drive!" I waved it at her. She opened one eye from where she sat on a plush chair, yawned, then closed her eyes again. "Okay. Not impressed, huh?"

I gave Rick a hug goodbye, then went upstairs to take a nap before work.

~

I WAS LAYING ON MY BACK IN BED, SLEEPING PEACEFULLY, dreaming about something lovely, when I heard a bird-like trill. Next thing I knew, Clover landed on my stomach with all fours.

"*Oof!*" I said.

She's a tiny thing, but that always knocks the breath out of me a bit.

She started kneading me with her cute little paws, purring heavily. Her eyes closed half-way as she got into the groove.

I rubbed her flanks with both hands, enjoying the rare cuddly moment with my high-energy cat. Then the moment was over. She meowed loudly, and I knew it was time for me to feed her.

I looked at my clock. And get to work! I'd slept through my alarm. Again.

I gently nudged Clover off of my chest, got out of bed, and got dressed for work.

As the owner of the Lucky Clover Tennis Shop, I got to decide what employees wore. I wasn't what you'd call a girly girl. My mom called me a Tomboy. So my employees and I wear uniforms. Cute green polo shirts with the shop logo, and crisp white or black pants. Because who looks good in shamrock-green pants?

I took Clover's cat carrier out of the closet and went downstairs with her following close behind me.

She may not have been impressed with Rick's cat-shaped flash drive, but the carrier got her attention! She loved going to the tennis shop with me. I dished up her wet cat food and she started rolling around on the floor in excitement.

"I know, I know. Hang on!" I grabbed her harness from a hook on the kitchen wall and put it on her while she was distracted by food. She looked so darn cute with a hot pink harness against her black and white fur. She purred as I lifted her into the top-loading carrier.

I carried her down to the car and opened my garage door just in time to see my widowed neighbor, Mrs. Chan.

"Hi, Mrs. Chan!" I said with a smile.

"Is that you, Madeline dear?" she asked, in her crinkly old-lady voice.

"Yes, Mrs. Chan. It's Madeline. Just going to work with my cat." I held up the carrier so she could see for herself. I could never tell how much Mrs. Chan could hear or see, but I wanted to be polite just in case.

"That's nice, dear," she said, then shuffled back toward her front door. She had the unit in the middle.

I put Clover into the front seat of my car and strapped the carrier in using specially-designed strap holders. I opened the top of the carrier so Clover could pop her head up and look out the window.

"Let's go have some fun!" I said.

"Meow!" she agreed.

As we drove the short ride to my tennis shop, Clover sat in her carrier with her little, white-mitten paws placed daintily on the side of the carrier. Her head stuck up just high enough for her to see out the passenger-side window. She meowed at the things going by - cars, people, dogs... she loved it.

We arrived at the shop around three o'clock, which was later than usual. There are certain benefits to being the owner. And thankfully I had an excellent assistant manager, Nikki. She was a creative type, with short curly hair (the color of which changed every few weeks - currently it was lime green), and several tattoos on her arms including a cupid with a bow and arrow on her right arm, and a cartoonish devil on her left. Nikki saw Clover and me walking toward the glass front doors and she ran up to open them for us.

"Hey, Boss!" she said, taking Clover's carrier from me.

"Hey, Nikki! Thanks. How has it been today? Busy? Quiet?" I asked.

"Oh, it was super busy!" Nikki said. She sat Clover's carrier on the floor and the cat immediately hopped up onto her sunny perch which was attached to one of the windows. "The tournament has everyone wanting to take up tennis. Thankfully, you have a pretty great back stock of most of the best-selling items. We are, however, running low on the beginners' rackets."

"Uh, oh. Well, I guess that's a nice problem to have," I said. I pulled a computer tablet out of a drawer and brought up my supplier's website. I entered a replacement order for the rackets, then did a sweep around the sales floor looking for other low-stock items while Nikki deftly handled a new influx of customers.

A FEW HOURS LATER, I SAID MY GOODBYES TO NIKKI AND packed up Clover for the trip home. Clover was always super-popular with the customers, especially with her little shamrock-green collar and four-leaf clover name tag.

I was just pulling into my driveway when Lizzy pulled up in her red Honda Civic.

"Hello, ladies!" she said to Clover and me as we got out of the car.

"Hello yourself!" I said.

"Meow," Clover echoed.

I took Clover out of her carrier, so she could head up the stairs. I followed Clover, with Lizzy at the back, closing the garage door behind us. "Let's get dinner started," she said. "I'm starving!"

In the kitchen, Clover went straight for her food while Lizzy opened a bottle of wine.

"Gotta get the most important ingredient open!" Lizzy said.

"Chicken Marsala doesn't take Cabernet!" I said. I opened the fridge and pulled out a bag which held two chicken breasts. I set them on the cutting board and carefully cut them in half horizontally, then began pounding on the chicken breasts.

"I know that, silly. That's for the chef and her best friend." She handed me a glass of wine. Then she opened a bottle of Marsala wine. "And this is for the meal."

AFTER DINNER, WE SAT ON THE BALCONY WITH OUR WINE, smelling the fresh ocean air and watching the sunset. I told her about the photos I had seen with Rick.

"Tomorrow, I want to pay a visit to Coach Masayuki to ask him what they were really arguing about," I said. I took a sip of wine and sighed in contentment. Clover sat on my lap. We kept each other warm in the cool night air.

"I *would* suggest that you leave that to the cops, but I know you'll just ignore me," Lizzy said.

"True," I said. She gave me a look. "What? You brought it up."

"Yeah, but you didn't have to agree with me so easily," she said, frowning. "Well, if you're going to investigate on your own, you may as well visit Brandon too."

"Who?" I asked.

"Brandon. The pickleball picketer."

"Oh! I didn't know you knew him. Why didn't you tell me this at the tournament?" I asked.

"Because, I don't *know* him, exactly," Lizzy said. "I know *of* him. Recently, he has started to make a lot of noise about pickleball."

"Huh. Okay. Any idea where I can find him?" I asked.

Lizzy scratched her chin in thought. "Hmm. Well, usually I see him at the tennis courts in town. Doing his picketing thing. Or I guess you could walk down Ventura Boulevard, ask about him in some of the shops there."

I nodded in agreement. "Speaking of shops, I need to spend some time at my own store tomorrow. Nikki needs some time off. She's been working hard. I'll have to wait until my lead salesperson Katie relieves me before I go talk to these guys." As the owner of my own tennis shop, I had the right to show up - or not - at my own discretion. But I tried to be considerate to my employees, and to me that meant showing up at least five days a week out of seven like they did.

"Good luck, *Detective* Quinn," Lizzy said, holding out her glass for a clinking.

"Ha ha. Very funny." Mildly annoyed at being called out, I clinked glasses anyway.

"In other news," I said, "You will never guess who I saw yesterday." I waggled my eyebrows provocatively and took a coy sip of my wine.

"Okay, I'll bite. Who?" Lizzy asked.

"Jeremy. Freaking. Miller." Mic drop.

"Who?"

"Oh, come on! You know. Jeremy, from-"

Before I could finish my rant, she started to laugh.

"Of course I know who Jeremy is," Lizzy said. "You were gaga for him for the first half of high school. Where'd you see him? I thought he'd moved away for college."

"He did. Studied forensics. I saw him at the coach's crime scene."

"And?! Tell me everything!" Lizzy said, pouring more wine. By now the sun had set, so we moved back inside. Clover curled up on her favorite chair.

"Well, he looked better than ever. He's so tall and buff..." my voice trailed off as my mind wandered.

Lizzy cleared her throat. "Come back to me, Mads."

"Ah! Sorry," I laughed self-consciously. "Anyway, I saw him again when I went in to give my statement." My face darkened at the memory of that morning.

"Why the long face all of a sudden?" she asked.

I told her how the conversation with Detective Dougan went and how I ran into Jeremy afterwards and made a fool of myself.

"I doubt Jeremy saw it that way. But I can't believe your sister let the detective put you through that!" she said angrily.

"Well, she had good reason, I guess, but yeah. That hurt, if I'm being totally honest."

"Of course it did. Sounds like he treated you like a suspect!"

"Yeah. But Annabelle said it was to prove that I wasn't getting any special treatment as her sister. The worst part was that I didn't even get Jeremy's number!" I said. "At the crime scene he said he wanted to see me again. Then he was so nice to me at the station after my interview. I don't want to have to hunt him down at work again. I especially don't want to have to ask Annabelle. That would be awkward on multiple levels."

"You'll figure it out, Mads," Lizzy said with a dismissive wave of her hand. "I have faith in you."

"Yeah, I'm sure you're right."

Chapter Three

Tuesday, September 30

As it turned out, he found me. Tuesday, while Clover and I were hard at work, I got a call from an unknown number on my personal cell phone. Unlike most people, I always answer these calls. My curiosity compels me to.

"Hello, this is Madeline," I said, as I rang up a customer. I smiled and handed her a large bag filled with a sky-blue tennis backpack, gloves, grip tape, and some Wilson US Open tennis balls.

"Hello, *Madeline*," a deep, warm voice said.

The happy tingles that went up and down my spine at the sound of his voice told me exactly who this was.

"I'm sorry, who is this?" I asked, though the sound of my voice betrayed the lie.

Jeremy ignored my silly question. Smart man. "Do you have any plans for lunch?" he asked.

"Uh, yes, sorry. I have to work. But how about dinner? Tonight at seven?"

"It's a date. Shall I pick you up? Or do you want to meet up somewhere?"

"Let's meet. Text me where and when and I'll be there with bells on." I rolled my eyes at myself. Ugh. Way to play it cool, Mads.

I could hear the laughter in his voice when he said, "Sounds good! Talk later."

Hanging up, I jumped up and down with a happy squeal. "I have a date!" I told Clover. She opened one eye at me in congratulations.

Thankfully, the store was uncommonly empty when my little outburst happened.

I WAS STARTING TO GO A BIT STIR CRAZY BY THE TIME KATIE arrived at the store to relieve me. Katie is a sweet lady in her mid-fifties. As an empty-nester with four grown children, my store was the perfect distraction from a quiet house.

"Hey Katie! Thanks for covering for me. Can you keep an eye on Clover, too? I don't want to have to drag her around town while I hunt down Brandon."

Katie looked at me sideways, as she gave Clover's head a loving scritch. "And Brandon is...?"

"He's a guy I saw arguing with Coach Matteo during the tournament," I said. "I just want to ask him about it."

"I'm more than happy to mind the store and to hang out with Clover," Katie said. "But are you sure you want to do this? Shouldn't you leave the 'hunting down' of people to your sister and her people?"

"Maybe 'hunting' wasn't the right word," I said, backpedaling a bit. "I'm just looking for him so I can ask him a few questions."

She didn't appear convinced, but still she said, "Okay, well, good luck."

I gave Clover a kiss on her furry little head, grabbed my purse, and headed out the door.

My tennis shop was on Ventura Boulevard. On that street, you'd find restaurants, bakeries, ice cream shops, antique stores, gift stores, and a little bookstore with a cafe. I figured I should start there. Get myself a chai tea latte and a snack to fortify myself for the walk.

A small collection of wind chimes announced my arrival at Cove Corner Books. The owner, Marcy Goodwin, popped up from behind the counter. She peered at me over her bifocals and smiled when she saw it was me.

"Mads! So good to see you! Can I get you your regular chai latte and a chocolate scone?"

"Heck yeah, you can! Thanks!" I ambled slowly up to the counter as I pulled out my wallet. It was always hard for me to walk past the book displays Marcy had between the door and the register.

She started making my tea and gave me a knowing wink. "See any books you like?"

"Always," I said with a sigh. "But there are only so many hours in a day."

Marcy handed me my scone so I could munch on it while I waited for my tea.

"Mmm. Blissfully good scone!" I said. She finished making my latte and slid it over.

I took the top off so I could inhale the spicy smell of the chai. I closed my eyes in pleasure. "Ahh." When I gathered my thoughts and opened my eyes, I found Marcy looking at me patiently. Apparently, I was the only one in the store at the moment.

"Sorry, got lost in the moment, there." I blushed, then cleared my throat. "So I came here for a specific purpose, not just the yummy snacks and a book. But first I have to know what you're doing for Sycamore Cove's Fall Harvest Festival that's coming up next month!"

She clapped her hands together in excitement. "Oh yes! I'm going to have some newly released books out, of course, but this year I want to have a book donation aspect as well. Maybe a few bins where folks can get rid of books they no longer want. I'm honestly not really sure how well this will work. It's not like people want to come to a festival lugging a bunch of books with them. But it's worth a shot, I suppose." She shrugged and gave me a small smile.

I nodded in understanding. "Yeah, that might be a tough sell, but if you let people know about it early enough, maybe have sign here at your shop or something, people can plan ahead and not be surprised by it."

"I like that, Mads. Thanks for the suggestion!"

"You bet! Now for my question... do you know a pickle-ball player named Brandon? You may have seen him arguing with Coach Matteo at the tournament? I'm trying to find him without driving to every tennis court in town."

"I'm sorry, Mads, but I don't. But you know I'm probably one of the few people in town that doesn't play tennis."

I chuckled at this. "Yes, I do know that. And I promise that I don't hold it against you!"

She placed her hand over her heart in exaggerated relief. "Oh, thank god."

"Okay, well, it was worth a shot. If only to get my chai and scone!" I said. "Next time I see you, I have some rare books I want to special order."

Marcy rubbed her hands together in anticipation. "Ooh! Can't wait to hear what you're getting! I love seeing rare books come through my store."

By now I had finished my food, so Marcy took my trash and threw it away behind the counter for me.

"Good luck on your quest for your pickle man!" Marcy said.

"Thanks!" I said, laughing my way out the door. Ha! *Pickle man.*

It was a beautiful day, so I took my time strolling up the street, past the yogurt shop and toward the crosswalk that led to the antique shop across the street. The cars stopped politely for a few other pedestrians, so I sped up a bit to cross with the small crowd. I waved and smiled at a few folks that I recognized.

As I reached the other side, I made a right at the sidewalk. A few stores down, I came upon one of our town's antique shops, Sycamore Antiques & Curios owned by Henry Whitcombe. Of all of the antique stores in our town, this was my favorite. He not only carried traditional antiques like old wood dressers, lamps, and Victorian couches, he also had some pretty cool "artifacts" from Egypt, Assyria, Rome, and other archaeological sites around the world. Most were replicas, I would imagine, but they still sparked my interest of all things mysterious.

I approached the front door just as one of the patrons came out. He held the door for me with a smile. I didn't immediately see Henry, so I gave myself some time to peruse the shop while I waited. My favorite section was the Egyptian artifacts. Especially the statues of cats. History suggests that Egyptians worshiped cats. They had the coolest names like Sekhmet, Bastet, and Mefdet. Maybe if I ever rescue a sibling for Clover, I could name it-

"Mads!" Henry called out as he appeared out of the back room. "Sorry, I was looking for a particular mirror for a customer. What can I do for you? You here to buy another cat statue?"

I laughed at this. He knew me so well!

Henry was a soft-spoken English man, whose hair had

gone quietly gray. He loved to wear cardigan sweaters and always had the faint scent of lemon oil and dust about him. One of the hazards of working with antiques all day, I suppose.

"No cat statue for me today, Henry! But now that I'm here, I realize that you likely won't have an answer for me. I'm looking for a pickleball player named Brandon. But now that I think about it, he doesn't strike me as the type that hangs out in antique shops. I think I just wanted an excuse to come in here." I smiled as I lovingly stroked a beautiful statue of Bastet. It was about a foot tall, and looked like it was made of brass with a beautiful blue-green patina. "Oh, man. I could fill my entire home with your cat collection."

Henry had the habit of listening before he spoke, head tipped slightly as if the shop itself were whispering to him. Now, he just gave a quiet chuckle. "I'd be on board with that! But I'll do you a favor and get you out of here quickly. I do not know any pickleball players, let alone a particular one named Brandon."

"I figured," I said. "Will I see any of your antiques at the Fall Harvest Festival?" That would be so cool! Statues, old mirrors, lamps, and lots of cat statues. Hopefully on sale.

"I'm afraid not. I'll be in England visiting my mum," he said.

"That's too bad. About you not having a booth. Not about you visiting your mom! I hope you have a nice time with her. Anyway, I'm gonna run over to the bakery now. That seems more like Brandon's style." I headed toward the door, then turned back. "Actually... would you please put a hold on that cat? I just love it."

"Done."

I could hear his chuckling again as I left his shop. I really needed to stop coming here.

My next and last stop for today was the bakery, Maison

du Croissant, or "House of the Croissant." I didn't want to leave Katie minding the shop - and Clover - for too long. And I'd already worked up another appetite for something sweet. Good thing I was getting in all of this walking!

I entered the small bakery and was greeted by a gust of air blowing in my face. It stopped once I crossed the threshold. The owner, Juste Blanchet, told me that it was to keep flies out of his shop. Made sense to me, and I always appreciated germ-free food.

His cozy little store had three small bistro tables with just two chairs each. It seemed he wanted people to be able to sit and eat, but not want to stay too long. As it was, all three tables were occupied and there was a small crowd of about five people waiting to order. I pulled a number from the little dispenser on the counter and gazed lovingly at the selection of treats: croissants, of course (as the name promised), but also apple turnovers, meringue cookies, lemon tarts, and my favorite, the canelé - a caramelized custard pastry. How to choose? To placate the American palate, Juste also carried donuts, albeit donuts with a French touch.

When it finally came my turn, I ordered some lemon tarts and six canelés. Hey. They're small!

"*Bonjour*, Mads! *Comment ça va?*" Juste asked.

"*Bonjour*, Juste! I'm well, thanks. Looks like business is thriving!"

"*Oui!* I can't complain."

"I know you're busy, so I won't keep you. I'm looking for a pickleball player named Brandon. Do you happen to know him or where I could find him today?" I hadn't had much success so far today, so I kept my hope in check.

To my surprise, Juste nodded. "*Oui.* He came in yesterday afternoon and bought a dozen of my American donuts." I saw Juste's mouth quickly twitch in distaste. "He has been coming in here every afternoon for more than a week to buy donuts.

He says they're for his 'pickle parties' at the courts on Temple. Whatever that means."

I was so shocked it took me a moment to respond. "Oh! Wow. Great! That's exactly what I needed to know. Thanks, Juste! And thank you for the treats. Hey, will you have a booth at the Fall Festival?"

"*Absolument.* It is the perfect opportunity for me to introduce my winter pastries and breads."

"I can't wait to see what you've come up with this year!" I said, nearly hopping up and down on my toes in my excitement. I really did love his baking.

"Thanks again for the info, Juste. See you later!"

He waved goodbye and turned to serve the new crowd forming behind me.

Enough of chasing down suspects. I needed to get ready for my first date with Jeremy!

I headed back to the tennis shop to grab Clover and head home to shower and change clothes. All of that walking got me a bit sticky.

At home, I refreshed Clover's water and food, then jogged upstairs to shower. But first, I wanted to figure out what I was going to wear. Oh, my. This could take a while. What does a girl wear on a date with her high school crush?

I was standing at the foot of the bed staring at five different outfits I had laid out when Clover joined me in the bedroom.

"Meow," she said, licking a paw and running it over her ear.

"I know, I know. But I can't decide!" I said.

Clover hopped up on the bed, walked back and forth a bit, then sat like a statue behind the black jeans, warm brown sweater, with adorable leather boots. Yup. The perfect choice for a cool fall evening.

"Great choice, Clover!"

"Meow," she agreed. She gracefully jumped off the bed and went to take a nap in a comfy chair while I showered.

As I got ready, I kept telling myself that there was no reason to be nervous. Jeremy and I were both adults now. We got along great, so far. There were no expectations for tonight.

My stomach, however, did not agree with this assessment. So I rummaged through my medicine cabinet for a Pepto-Bismol. I also took an antacid just to cover all of my bases. If I weren't getting ready to drive myself to the restaurant, I would have had a glass of wine, as well.

As it was, I gave Clover a scritch goodbye and headed down to the car.

JEREMY AND I MET UP AT A CUTE LITTLE ITALIAN RESTAURANT that I'd never been to before. We ordered some wine, chose some amazing-sounding meals, then proceeded to catch up with each other after eight plus years of being apart. Though, to be fair, we were never really together. I just had a major crush on a guy two grades ahead of me.

"So yeah," Jeremy said a while later. "After school, I worked for a local sheriff's department near school. With forensics, your career path is fairly set if you do things right. You start out as a trainee, then move up through the levels after a year or more at each level. I'm now a level three. Just started when I moved back here." He took the last bite of his gnocchi in meat sauce.

"Wow. Congrats!" I said. "Sounds like you're really enjoying forensics."

He nodded. "Yeah. It can be grueling sometimes, and gruesome, but I really feel like I'm making a difference. It's very rewarding work. And how about you? I think we've heard enough about me."

I took a sip of my wine to give me time to gather my thoughts. He's out there, helping solve crimes, "making a difference." What do I have to offer?

"Well, I have my own little tennis pro gear shop. You may recall I've always had a passion for tennis. For most of high school, I played in juniors tennis, which is organized tennis for kids under eighteen. I had to give up my dreams of going pro when I seriously injured my knee. So when my grand-parents died and left me some money in their will, I opened my own store. Keeps me healthy and involved with tennis and with the community. It also brings in pretty good money. I may not have a fancy pension," I looked down at my food. "And maybe I'm not changing anyone's life, but I'm happy."

I was afraid to look up at him. Would he think my dreams of owning a little tennis shop were petty? Would he be disap-pointed in me?

After a moment of quiet, I felt him reach across the table and take my hands in his. "Hey," he said. I finally looked up into his eyes. "I happen to think you are amazing." He smiled at me and his eyes shone with pride. "It's no small task to start and own a business. The fact that you help people stay healthy, and that it's something you enjoy, is even better."

"I mean, it's not like I'm saving anyone's life or anything..." My eyes wandered away from him, searching for something to focus on.

"Stop. Madeline Quinn. Look at me," he said. He stopped talking until I looked at him again. "Don't sell yourself short. I won't allow it."

My eyes teared up and I smiled. How did he do that? He

just looks at me and I feel like the most amazing person in the world.

I cleared my throat, breaking the spell. "Anyway, hey. Speaking of tennis, what's going on with Coach Matteo's case?"

We had finished our meals and ordered desserts and cappuccinos.

"Hmm. Well, I shouldn't be sharing information with anyone outside the department, but I know and trust you will keep things confidential." He raised his eyebrows at me in question. "Right?"

"Huh? Oh, yes! Of course. Confidential," I said. I tried not to let on just how badly I wanted some information. Any information. It sucked being on the outside. I took a bite of my butter cake to keep my mouth shut and let him talk.

"The poor guy seemed pretty beat up," Jeremy said, sipping his coffee.

I nodded, as I thought about the odd markings on Coach's body. The ones that I had photographed at the crime scene. That and all the blood.

"Sometimes after a body has had some time to rest, bruising will show up that wasn't there before. Or, I should say, wasn't *visible* before. It *was* there," he said. He took another sip of coffee, and I had to hold tight onto my own coffee cup so as not to throttle more information out of him. That would not do good things for our budding relationship. Patience may be a virtue, but it's not one of mine. But I sure hoped that wasn't all he had to say. My silence was rewarded. Maybe I proved that I could be silent when needed.

"Looks like your coach sustained a black eye not long before his death. He also had a broken rib."

At this news, I dropped my coffee spoon loudly onto my saucer, causing some of the restaurant patrons to look my way. "Sorry," I mumbled, and picked up the spoon. "Wow. I didn't notice any of that when I found his body. Coach Matteo winced after I hugged him at the tournament, but he told me that his rib was bruised, not broken."

Jeremy shook his head. "No, you wouldn't have known it was broken just by looking at the body. Even if you knew what to look for, you'd need the right equipment to analyze the injured tissue, not to mention the experience to know how to interpret the results."

I nodded thoughtfully. Yeah. That made sense. Which reminded me...

"Jeremy, I have to show you something," I said. He looked at me curiously. "I know I probably shouldn't have done this, but I took photos of Coach Matteo's body right after I found him. I saw some very odd markings on his body." I took out my phone and showed Jeremy the photos I had taken. He nodded solemnly.

"Yes, I remember the medical examiner mentioning it. She's not yet sure what caused these marks, but they will be a part of the investigation just like the black eye and the broken rib."

"I wonder if Brandon is the one who killed him," I said. "Maybe he came back later, after the tournament, wanting revenge for being humiliated."

"Brandon?"

"Yes. He's the picklegate guy. My brother Rick has photos of their fight at the tournament. It seemed pretty serious."

"Picklegate?" Jeremy laughed. "Well, I'd like to see those photos as well, when you get the chance, though maybe not over dinner. Though really, you should show them to Detective Dougan," he said.

The waiter brought our check and Jeremy grabbed it before I could. "My treat," he said.

"I thought we'd go dutch," I said.

"Nope. I consider this a date and I'm an old-fashioned

guy." He looked me in the eyes. Wow. I never realized there was so much green in his hazel eyes. "And I hope it's just the first of many." He smiled.

My head went all fuzzy, and I smiled back. "I'd love that. Oh, and the detective should also look into Coach Masayuki. I hate to even think about him doing something like this, but they also really got into it."

Way to completely ruin the moment, Mads.

I also hated giving away my suspect ideas, but I was pretty sure I could get some time to ask them some questions before the police got around to it.

As we'd met at the restaurant, Jeremy walked me to my car when our date was over. The evening was cool, with a gentle breeze that ruffled my hair. Jeremy smiled and used a finger to carefully wrap a stray lock of hair behind my ear. "I love the color of your hair. It's like a sunset."

Oh my god. That was so romantic! I gave him a shy smile and tucked my chin into my shoulder.

Jeremy lifted my chin so I was looking up at him.

"I..." he started. His eyes searched mine earnestly.

When he didn't continue, I prompted him. "Yes? You... what?"

"I just don't want to rush things," he said. "What with how long it has been since we've seen each other, and the murder, and all..."

My smile faltered.

"And we never even really dated in high school. I want to do this right. Get to know each other properly. As adults that want to date." He paused. "We do want to date, right?" he asked, eyebrows raised in question.

At this, I was surprised to find a touch of relief. No pressure. We could take our time.

"It's not that I don't want to kiss you, Maddie. Please know that. In fact, it's taking quite a bit of willpower."

I let out a breath I didn't know I was holding. "Yes! Yes, we do want to date. And I want to do things right," I said.

He stepped back just a bit. "You sure are beautiful, Maddie," he said.

"You are, too," I said. I chuckled then blushed in embarrassment. "Sorry. That sounded-"

"Thank you," he said. "I'll take that compliment. Is it too soon in our relationship to ask you to text me when you get home safely?"

"No, it's not. I will. Goodbye, Jeremy," I said, grinning like a love-struck idiot.

Chapter Four

Wednesday, October 1

The next day, I took the morning off work so I could have a chat with my two suspects.

"I'm sorry, Clover. I need to leave you here for now. I think you'd be bored."

"Meow," she said.

"I'll take that as an, 'okay mom!'," I said. She didn't look convinced.

I headed down to the garage, and as soon as I opened the garage door, I could smell the ocean air. Definitely a great day to own a convertible, I thought, as I opened up my top. I told myself I needed to make time for the beach soon. I'd been super-focused on prepping for the tournament the past few weeks.

As I drove, I sang along to old eighties tunes. My mother's favorite. A few minutes of side roads and belting out Duran Duran's "Hungry Like the Wolf" and "Save a Prayer" I arrived at the tennis courts where the tournament was held. I knew this was where Coach Masayuki gave lessons. He had so many students, he was bound to be there in the middle of any given morning.

And I wasn't disappointed. I parked away from the bird-filled trees and made my way toward the courts. Sure enough, there he was with his star pupil, no less. Courtney Engelmann.

I watched her practice her serve and was duly impressed. I'm known for my killer serve, but this girl was truly an ace. She hit it down the T every time.

"Hmm. She's really good," I said out loud to no one. Maybe now that I'm coach-less, I should sign up with Coach Masayuki. And soon. Before he gets too busy from being famous. He may not even be taking new students.

"Okay, Courtney," Coach Masayuki said. "That's fantastic footwork. Let's take a short water and bathroom break. Then we'll work on your backhand."

"Yes, Coach," she said. She walked over to her bag and grabbed a face towel to wipe off her sweat. She took a long swig of water and waved at me.

"Hey, Courtney!" I said, waving back.

I watched Coach Masayuki walk toward the restrooms. They'd long since cleaned up and released the crime scene.

If he did kill Coach Matteo, I'll bet it feels weird being at the scene of one's own crime!

I figured I'd better let him use the restroom before I tried to ask him any questions. Don't want his eyes swimming while I'm trying to get information!

Courtney took the opportunity to go to the women's room while I waited for Coach Masayuki. Finally, he came out. He was still wiping his hands on a paper towel.

As that was an indication of good hygiene, I approached him with my hand out. He tossed his paper towel in the trash and took my hand to shake it.

"Hello, Madeline! It's nice to see you. What are you doing here? What with... well, you know... you not having a coach and all..." he trailed off awkwardly, cheeks reddening. "I'm sorry. That was rude."

Courtney came out of the restroom and he waved her toward their court. "Be right there!" he said. She nodded and went to wait for him.

"So, is there something I can help you with? I'm afraid I'm not taking any new students right now, if that's what you-"

"No, no," I said, stopping him. "Um, actually, I wanted to ask you about the argument you had with Coach Matteo at the tournament."

At this, his whole demeanor changed.

"Frankly, I don't see how that is any of your business," he said. "I need to get back to my lesson."

Coach Masayuki went back to the court, and I could see that they were talking about me. Sigh.

I hung out of sight until they were done. I went into the women's locker room to wait for Courtney. When she walked in and saw me, she stopped short.

"I'm sorry, Madeline, I'm not supposed to talk to you," she said, pushing past me toward the lockers.

"Call me Mads," I said. Like that would solve everything. "Wait. Why aren't you allowed to talk to me? Why the secrecy? Does Coach Masayuki have something to hide?"

She looked uncomfortable. "I don't know. He just asked me not to talk to you. Look, I really don't know anything, okay?"

I could tell from the look on her face that's all I'd be getting out of her. I sighed. Well, maybe I'll have better luck with Brandon the pickleball guy.

~

NOPE. NO SUCH LUCK.

As Juste had suggested, I found Brandon at the Temple

courts, once again picketing with his sign. This time, there were three of them - one guy, one girl, and Brandon. The box of donuts sat on a nearby bench. I approached their little group with a smile and wave.

"Hey, Brandon! Got a minute?" I asked.

He frowned in my direction, shaded his eyes from the sun with his free hand, then handed his sign to the gal that was with them. She now had a sign in each hand, and alternated their time being shoved into the air.

"Yeah? Who are you? What do you want?" he said.

Jeeze. Friendly guy.

"Well, I-"

"Wait. Are you with the press?" He smiled, and pointed at the box of donuts on the bench behind him. "I have some fantastic donuts from Maison du Croissant."

"No, I-"

"Oh. Do you want to join the protest? We want dedicated courts for pickleballers." He looked at my hands as though I might be hiding a sign somewhere.

Before he could interrupt me a third time, I quickly said, "What happened between you and Coach Matteo the other day?"

Brandon looked perplexed. "Do I know you? Who's Matteo?"

"No, you don't know me. We have a friend in common," I figured I wouldn't bother telling him who. He didn't seem to be listening to me anyway. "I saw the two of you fighting at the tournament. You were picketing, and he approached you. Seems like you had some angry words for each other."

"I have every right to picket!" He turned back toward the tennis players. "Pickleballers have rights, too! We deserve our own courts!" he yelled.

I cringed at the sudden change in volume.

He turned back to me with an "and?" look.

"And I wanted to know if you killed him," I asked. Ha! Take that! I was hoping I'd catch him by surprise and he'd confess.

"Wait, what? He's dead? When did *that* happen? Don't go blaming me for that!"

"We think-"

"No! I did not kill him. Didn't even *touch* him. Look. I gotta go. Kinda busy here," he said. With that, he grabbed his sign back and started yelling again.

Okay, then. Guess that conversation is over!

I turned to leave and noticed Denise Christensen was playing a game on one of the tennis courts. I waved to her, but I don't think she saw me.

BY THE TIME I GOT DONE WITH MY INTERROGATIONS, ER, conversations, it was getting late. I realized I had a dinner date with my family. I groaned to myself.

I loved my family dearly, but as the middle child, I always felt a bit forgotten. Rick's photography business was booming, and Annabelle... well, she was in a league of her own. But I truly enjoy the life I've made for myself, and in the end, that's all that matters!

I slipped on a summery dress, fed and scritched the cat, and with a sincere apology for ignoring her all day, drove to my parents' house.

My parents lived in a large, two-story English Tudor home with cream stucco, dark wood exposed beams, and a pitched gable roof. It looked like something out of a fairy tale. When I arrived, before I could even knock, I heard the barking of my mom's two little Shih Tzus behind the door. I heard a muffled, "Chloe! Gigi! Be quiet!"

Mom opened the door and the dogs stopped barking

once they saw it was only me. I bent to give them each a loving scritch on their adorable little heads. "Hello, you little cuties!" They did a short little dance hello, then wandered off to more interesting things.

"Hello, Madeline," Mom said. She was the only one that still called me that, and could only give me half of a hug as she had a glass of white wine in her hand. I followed her into the kitchen where I found my sister Annabelle sipping her own glass of white wine.

I slapped my head in annoyance. I had forgotten to bring my own wine. I hate white wine, but that's all my mom and sister drink. Sigh. Guess I was having soda tonight.

"That's a beautiful dress sweetheart," Mom said, looking me up and down. "Can I pour you a glass?" She held up her glass to indicate what she was offering.

"No thanks, Mom. I don't like white wine, remember?" She nodded slowly, as though she had remembered this all along, but was just being polite.

"Hey, Sis," I said, giving Annabelle a hug.

"Hey, Maddie," she said.

I looked around the kitchen for Annabelle's husband and my niece. "Where are Sean and Summer?" I asked.

"Sean took her camping," Annabelle said. "Things have gotten a bit busy at work, so we thought it best that he take her somewhere fun for a bit."

I nodded knowingly. I was dying to ask my sister about Coach Matteo's murder, but knew I couldn't attack her right away. Let her get some food and a few glasses of wine in her first.

"Where's Dad and Rick?" I asked, looking around. I set my purse on a kitchen chair and grabbed a Coke out of the fridge.

Mom widened her eyes at me. "You'll be up all night if you drink that now!"

"I'm used to them, Mom. I'm immune to the caffeine. It's the sugar and flavor I seek," I cracked open the can. I'd always loved that sound. Reminded me of opening a fresh can of tennis balls.

Thankfully, my brother and dad came in from outside in time to save me from more judgements about my beverage choices.

Apparently, they'd been in Dad's workshop. They were smiling and talking animatedly about some chairs my dad had made. He was a highly skilled woodworker, and now that he was retired, his passion had organically grown into a thriving business. He worked by commission only and had more business than he knew what to do with.

"Why don't you come by tomorrow, Rick, and take some photos for the website," Dad said. "I don't think we have any examples of high-back dining room chairs yet."

Rick nodded. "I may have to raise my prices though. Your business may be thriving, but mine is, too." Rick grabbed two beers out of the fridge and handed one to Dad.

Dad laughed and patted him heartily on the back. "How about we discuss that more tomorrow after our bike ride. Right now, it's time for dinner! Camille?" he asked my mom. "What's for dinner, dear?" He walked over to her and gave her a long kiss. Thirty-eight years of marriage and they still adored each other.

"Hello, Bobby, my love. We're having pot roast with potatoes *au gratin*," she smiled and gave him an affectionate pat on the butt.

Ew. Didn't need to see that.

My parents were in fantastic shape. As a Pilates goddess, my mom puts me to shame. I may be a tennis nut, but I still don't play as many times per week as I'd like. And unfortunately, I have thirty-two sweet teeth.

Mom dished up the plates and we all took our meals to the table.

After a long while catching up with each other, I figured it was finally time to let them know what I've been up to lately. I knew my sister didn't like to talk shop, but that didn't mean I couldn't bounce some ideas off of everyone. And while Annabelle wouldn't talk about open cases with us, I could read her like a book. I'd get a pretty good idea of how close I was getting with my short suspect list.

"So...," I started tentatively. "The other day, Rick and I were going through some of the photos from the tournament and saw some pretty interesting stuff." I paused to gauge the mood of the room.

My sister gave me a sharp look of warning. She knew exactly where I was headed.

Rick closed his eyes, shook his head, and sighed.

I know, I know. It wasn't fair to drag him into this, but why should I be the only weird one in the family? I wanted some company. Was that so wrong?

My mom and dad, always trying to be the supportive parents, glanced my way with non-committal, vaguely interested looks.

"Oh?" Mom asked.

Encouraged, I forged ahead quickly before I lost my nerve.

"Well, from what I saw in the photos, either Coach Masayuki or Brandon the pickleball guy could have had something to do with Coach Matteo's, um, demise."

For some reason, I couldn't bring myself to say "murder" at the family dinner table. Maybe it had something to do with the looks I was now getting from both siblings.

"Look, Maddie," Annabelle said. "We've spoken to both men about their possible motives and alibis and neither are a person of interest in this case. I can tell you this, because we're going to be holding a press conference tomorrow morning stating as much."

"But-" maybe there were things they didn't know.

"No 'buts' about it. I don't want you doing your Sherlock Holmes bit and harassing these men," Annabelle said, giving me her stern, policewoman look. It was formidable, I have to admit.

"I wasn't 'harassing' them," I said a bit more defensively than intended. "I asked a few reasonable questions that anyone might ask..."

Annabelle put her head in her hands and groaned.

"Madeline, your sister is right. You shouldn't be getting in the way of her doing her job," Mom said.

Now I was starting to take it personally. "I'm not getting in anyone's way. I'm just a private citizen having private conversations with people." I turned to Annabelle. "And did you know that Coach Matteo may have had his star player stolen from him by Coach Masayuki? Or that the pickleball guy claims he didn't so much as touch Coach Matteo, but that we have photographic proof to the contrary?" I looked around the table for vindication.

My sister, to her credit, at least looked thoughtful. Like she was absorbing this new information.

Rick reached into his pocket and pulled out a flash drive. "I brought you copies of the photos. They're all here, in case we missed something."

My sister reluctantly held out her hand for the drive. "Thank you, Rick," she said.

We all started to eat again, quietly, focused on our food.

"Well, you just might want to have a look at the photos before you announce to the world that they're innocent. Just sayin'," I mumbled into my plate of potatoes.

At that, I heard Annabelle audibly sigh.

Chapter Five

Thursday, October 2

The next morning, my sister held her press conference. As this was some of the biggest news our town had had in quite some time, Annabelle decided to also allow members of the community and not just the press to attend. It was also being televised. This allowed me to watch from home while I got ready for work. The camera panned the room, so I could see the crowd. It then panned back to the front of the room, waiting.

My sister stood grimly at the front of the police station's press room, hands on the podium, looking down at her notes while she waited for the room to quiet. The room was packed to the gills.

She looked up, and the room went silent with anticipation.

"For those of you that don't know me, my name is Annabelle Quinn Murphy, Chief of Police. We are here this morning to ask for the public's help regarding the murder of twenty-eight-year-old Matteo Amato. Before I begin, I would like to acknowledge some people who are here with me today. From our homicide department, we have

Detective Doug Dougan, and crime scene investigators Jeremy Miller and Fiorella Napolitani from our Crime Scene Investigation Unit.

"ALSO WITH ME TODAY ARE CAPTAIN HERRMANN AND Sergeant Liu, and our Sycamore Cove Mayor, Emma Mitchell.

"On September 26, 2025, at nine forty-five at night, our officers responded to a 911 call about a dead body at the Sycamore Cove Tennis Club. Upon arrival, Detective Dougan observed Mr. Amato near the men's restroom sinks. He appeared to be the victim of a fatal beating.

"The Ventura County Medical Examiner arrived on scene and pronounced Matteo Amato deceased.

"Homicide investigators learned that the murder likely occurred sometime after the Sycamore Cove Tennis Club's tournament where Mr. Amato had been a coach.

"At this time, we do not have any suspects in this case, so I would like to give special thanks to our County Supervisor for his approval of a ten thousand dollar reward for information leading to the arrest and conviction of the person, or persons, responsible for the murder of Matteo Amato. The victim's family in Italy has been notified.

"We won't be taking any questions at this time. Thank you."

Annabelle and her team started to leave the podium, so I switched off the TV.

I made particular note of the fact that my sister's press conference was absent of any references to Brandon's or Masayuki's innocence. I took that to mean that Annabelle was taking this - taking me - seriously.

I smiled and turned toward Clover to share the good news with her. She was sitting on top of the kitchen counter, next to the warm TV. Clover wasn't allowed on the counter, so of course that was one of her favorite spots. I had lost that battle a long time ago.

"Isn't that great, Clover? That I actually changed my big sister's mind about something?" I poured a hefty amount of heavy cream into my medium roast coffee. I was trying to quit sugar, but no amount of cream seemed to make up for that lack of sweetness.

"Meow," Clover dutifully said. She stood up and came toward me to rub her cheek and flank along my arm. Of course, it might just be that she wanted some cream.

"You know cats are lactose intolerant, Clover!" I chided.

"Meow," she said.

"Don't argue with me. Here, have a cat-friendly 'yogurt' tube instead." I grabbed a snack tube out of the plastic tub and fed it to a very happy cat.

After a long day working at the tennis shop, I knew I had to make time for some actual tennis.

Although I had won the matches I played during the first round of the tournament, I wasn't quite happy with my backhand. And thanks to our success at the tournament, there would be a second round of tournament matches tomorrow, which was all too soon. So I took my ball shooter and one hundred tennis balls, and headed to the tennis club courts.

It was later than I would usually practice when by myself, but I still had a few hours of sunlight left, and there were still quite a few people at the courts as well as the adjacent swimming pool.

I set my little machine on one side of the court and did a few minutes of warm-up exercises. No sense in pulling something right before a tournament day!

I turned the machine on, then took my place on the other side of the court. After a few moments, the machine started shooting balls in my direction. Sure enough, my first few minutes of backhands were pretty bad. But soon, I got into the rhythm of it.

As always happens to me with tennis, I found myself completely losing track of time. Next thing I knew, it was getting dark, so I packed up my gear and headed for the locker room restrooms.

Before Coach Matteo had died, I never had any concerns about being alone at the tennis club. But now I was looking around a bit nervously. Still, the lights were on and I really needed to go, so I dragged my gear into the bathroom.

I finished my business and was washing my hands when I started to smell a distinctly masculine scent - maybe after-shave. Whatever it was, it was not a scent that belonged in a women's locker room. It mingled a bit with the sterile-smelling deodorizer that would automatically spritz the locker rooms every few minutes to keep things smelling fresh.

As I turned off the water, I heard the *pfsst* sound of the deodorizer. A moment later there was a soft, but very male-sounding cough coming from the lockers nearby.

I froze in fear. Maybe I was overreacting, but it was late, dark, and I was alone.

I wiped my wet hands on my shirt and slowly and quietly reached for my phone which I always kept in a fanny pack when playing tennis. I may be considered brave by some standards, but I wasn't stupid. My phone was always charged and on my person.

Keeping an eye on where I'd heard the noise, I dialed 911 and put the phone to my ear.

"911, what's your emergency?"

"Yes," I whispered, backing away from the lockers. "This is

Madeline Quinn and I'm at the Sycamore Cove Tennis Club. I-"

Quick as a flash, a man wearing all black clothes and a full-face ski mask pushed past me, knocking me to the cold, tile floor. I fell hard with an "*Umph!*"

My phone flew out of my hand and skidded across the floor, ending up somewhere under the lockers. There was no way I could locate my phone *and* chase the guy down.

So, of course, I got up and raced after him.

"Hey! Stop!" I yelled at his retreating back. "Is anyone here? I could use some help, please!" I called out to the empty grounds.

This guy was moving fast! I could see him running toward the other end of the parking lot. I couldn't let him get to his car.

That's when I spotted the tennis club's golf cart. Perfect! Technically, tennis club guests weren't allowed to drive them. They were for employees only. But this was an emergency! And how hard could it be to drive a golf cart? They're practically self-driving, right?

Wrong.

I hopped into the driver's seat. Nothing happened. I looked around for a key or start button. It was getting pretty dark now, and I didn't see anything at first. I wasn't worried, though. As soon as I figured this out, I'd catch up to him in no time!

I reached for my phone to use it as a flashlight and cursed when I realized it was still on the bathroom floor somewhere.

"Augh!" I growled in frustration.

Finally, I spotted it. The key! It had two positions: on and off. I turned it to the on position. I pressed my foot to the "gas" pedal and the cart shot backward.

"Eek!" I yelled in shock. Seriously? Who leaves a cart in

reverse? I braked and noticed a toggle button next to the key. It said "FWD" and "REV." It was in reverse! I flipped the button to FWD and lurched ahead.

Finally! My quarry had made good progress, but I raced toward him.

A bit too fast.

My right tire caught the edge of the grass and pulled my cart off-balance. I tilted and lurched toward the right. The next thing I knew, I was being tossed out of the cart and knocked unconscious.

I woke to the lights of a variety of emergency vehicles.

"She's awake!"

Mmm. I liked the warm, soothing sound of that voice. He sounded familiar... Jeremy!

I blinked into the bright light of Jeremy's hand-held pen light. I squinted and raised my hand to protect my eyes.

"Hold still, Maddie. You've had quite a spill," Jeremy said.

He checked me over and cleared me of any major injury.

"Okay, you seem alright, but we should probably get you to a hospital," Jeremy said. Gently, he helped me to a standing position.

I waved him off impatiently. "No. No hospital. I'm fine. Oh!" I said, as it all started to come back to me. "The bad guy! Did you see where he went? Did you catch him?" I asked.

"Um, did you just say, 'bad guy'?" Jeremy tried to cover a laugh with a cough.

I listed sideways a bit and grasped Jeremy's shoulders. In part, to keep myself steady, but also to get his full attention.

Jeremy's eyes widened in alarm. "Woah! Slow down now." He looked at me with concern on his face.

"I'm okay, Jeremy. Really," I said. "But that guy was in the women's locker room looking for something. I'd like to know what it is, wouldn't you? Also, my phone and tennis stuff are still there. I need to go get it."

Jeremy nodded in understanding. He had the EMT give me an official exam and release, and the ambulance left. Jeremy then had a quick chat with the two officers who had responded to the scene and the four of us went together to the locker room.

I led them to where I thought the guy had been hiding.

"He was here, I think," I said, taking them to the second row of lockers.

Despite the unsanitary nature, I got down onto the tile floor to look under the lockers. I reached my hand out to Jeremy. "Can I borrow your flashlight, please? Oh, and can you call my phone? It's a bit dark under there."

I heard my phone buzz against the tile. Thankfully, it hadn't been on silent. I could see it, but it was out of reach. I stood up.

"I need something long to knock it out from under there. Could you help me look around for a broom or something?" I asked.

"Hey," Jeremy said. "I think I see something stick-like on top of that locker. Let me see if I can..." He started jumping up and down, trying to knock the stick off the locker. Grunting a bit with effort, he said, "Yes! I- think- I- got-" his fingers hit the side of the stick, and it came tumbling down to the floor.

All four of us looked down in shock at the bent, bloody tennis racket that now lay at Jeremy's feet.

"Aw, crap," Jeremy said. "I think I just moved the murder weapon."

With a look of chagrin on his face, he said, "Maddie, you need to go home and get some rest. You don't have to go to the hospital. The EMT gave you a clean bill of health. But you don't have to stay while I process the scene. It will take a while."

I was exhausted, so it was hard to argue. But something caught my eye.

"Jeremy! Does that look like another one of those hairs I saw near Matteo's body?" I pointed to a long silvery hair stuck in the matted blood on the tennis racket.

He looked back at me, eyes wide. "Good eye, Maddie!" He smiled at me, and I almost had enough of a burst of dopamine from that smile to make me want to stay.

Almost.

I FELT PRETTY STIFF AFTER MY EVENTFUL NIGHT AT THE TENNIS club. I'd practiced for two hours and then got knocked around and tossed out of a golf cart!

Finally home, I slowly made my way upstairs to my kitchen.

No matter how I was feeling, Clover still needed to be cared for. It wasn't her fault that I could barely move. Not to mention I'd been gone for much longer than planned. By the time Jeremy told me to go home, I had been gone close to six hours. I should have called Lizzy and asked her to look in on Clover hours ago.

Clover let me know how she felt by pretending I wasn't there. But I gave her fresh food, water, and then made amends by waving her favorite treats under her nose. This got me a leg rub and loud purr.

Forgiven by my cat, I scarfed a microwave burrito then poured myself a tall glass of one of my own favorite treats - Josh Cabernet - and slowly made my way up the second set of stairs to the bedroom. I really needed to put some thought into getting a one-story home.

As I ran the bath, I thought about who could've been in the locker room with me tonight. It couldn't have been a tournament player, as we're all women. The racket has to have been what the man was looking for. If all he wanted was something innocent, like an item of clothing, why wear a mask? But who did the racket belong to? And for that matter, who did *he* belong to? If there were no male players in our tournament, what was he doing in the women's locker room looking for a racket?

I slowly and gratefully sank into the hot bubble water. I sipped my wine and relaxed my mind, letting it wander.

Too bad I didn't get a kick or punch in when the guy passed by. Instead, I got knocked to the floor like a child. My left arm was already starting to bruise. Sigh.

Tomorrow was round two of the tournament, and there would be another party. I'd need to have a good look at all of the men there.

Chapter Six

Thursday, October 2

It was finally Friday! Time for the tournament playoffs. We were all gathered in the open-air court for pep talks and instructions.

One would think that we'd have moved the tournament to another location, considering the coach's murder and the discovery of the bloody racket.

However, ours was a small town. First of all, we only had one tennis facility large enough to house a tournament. Second of all, except for the Fall Harvest Festival, this tournament was the biggest event our town saw all year. Therefore, both the mayor (Lizzy's mom) and the chief of police (my sister) were in complete agreement that the crime scenes should be released, and the show should go on.

Besides, the murder took place in a public locker room. Any DNA and prints taken from the scene of the crime were virtually useless. Same story for the bloody racket. The racket itself was currently with forensics, but the rest of the scene was again too public to be useful. Also, they had decided to keep the finding of the potential murder weapon a secret for now. That would have been harder to do with crime scene tape all over the place.

So here we all were, ready for another round.

Once again, Lizzy and I sat together on one of the large, grass-covered steps of the sunken tennis court.

Coach Masayuki was giving everyone the same set of rules that we'd heard from Coach Matteo on the first day.

"I wonder if coaches get paid for running these things," I whispered to Lizzy.

"Maybe," she said. "But I can't imagine it's all that much. Certainly not worth killing for?"

"Yeah, you're probably right." She had a point.

Denise sat down next to us on the step. She plopped her tennis bag onto the step in front of us, next to ours.

"Hey!" I said. Where's your racket?" I noticed a definite lack of a racket handle popping out of the top or side of her bag.

"Oh! I guess my mom must have it," she said, unworried.

"The tournament is going to start soon. You'd better make sure!" Lizzy said.

"You're right. Thanks for letting me know. I don't know where my head is today. I guess I just really miss Coach Matteo." She grabbed her bag and stood up.

As she walked past me, I noticed some odd brown stains near the top opening of the bag. I gasped and elbowed Lizzy. She looked at me curiously, eyebrows raised. I gave her a quick shushing look and waited until Denise was out of earshot.

"Did you see that?" I asked.

"What?" she asked.

"That looked like blood on Denise's bag!" My eyes wide, I looked at Lizzy in shock.

"Blood? From what?"

"Exactly!"

"Maybe she hurt herself?" Lizzy said. "Wait. Are you sure it was blood?" she asked.

I sighed. "Well, I suppose it could be something else, but it looked like blood to me!" I stared at Lizzy in disbelief. "Do you think..." I stopped when I noticed quite a few people giving me the evil eye. "Sorry!" I whispered.

We sat quietly and listened to the rest of the instructions.

A few minutes later, I spotted my brother Rick wandering around taking photos. We gave each other a nod. I had tasked him with taking more photos than usual, and with a particular eye toward getting photos of all of the males in attendance. Thanks to Jeremy, I now knew that Coach Matteo had a black eye as well as a broken rib and was beaten pretty badly in general. Plus, it was definitely a guy that knocked me over in the women's locker room. Though what he was doing there still bothered me. Anyway, I was hoping Rick's photos would capture something telling.

Finally, it was time to play! We filed toward the draft table to find out who we'd be playing.

"Aw, crap," I said. "Once again, it looks like I could end up playing Tracy!" My heart sank.

Lizzy gave me a sympathetic look. "I think you and I need to start practicing with a left-handed player. Just to prep for next year's tournament."

"Good idea," I said. I was still sore from my golf cart mishap the night before, and now this? I found myself wishing for the hundredth time that Jeremy could be here. I assumed he was working on the racket findings, which would certainly be more important than a few games of tennis. Still...

I saw my parents arrive without my sister, but her husband Sean and my niece, Summer, were with them. I suppose Annabelle also had duties related to the murder. I waved to my family who smiled and waved back.

Hours later, I had won all of my matches in straight sets, except for the one against Tracy. I won the first set, but Tracy came back hard and won the second. Luckily, I won the third set, thus winning the match.

Thankfully she was my last match of the day, so all in all, I felt pretty good about the day. Lizzy had also fared well, though not as well as I had.

My parents came by to congratulate me with hugs and kisses.

I'll never be too old for that.

AFTER THE AWARDS CEREMONY, LIZZY AND I WENT TO MY house for clean-up and cat duties. We then headed out to Pop's Pizza for the final party. We had won the tournament again, thus securing first place for Sycamore Cove in the SoCal National Championships.

Despite the win, the celebration was more subdued this time. I could hear people whispering about Coach Matteo's death. I, too, got a lot of stares, having found the body. I could tell people wanted to ask me about it but were being polite. Unfortunately, it wasn't the first time I'd been in a situation like this, so I didn't take it personally. I just hoped that finding bodies wouldn't become a thing for me.

I tried hard to look at all of the men for any odd behavior toward me. I knew the person in the locker room was a man, and figured whoever had encountered me last night might be acting strangely toward me. I also knew he was taller than my five foot seven inches, but I couldn't just walk up to every male taller than me and sniff him for bad aftershave choices. That move would likely get a bunch of wives angry at me.

And thanks to the whole "Coach Matteo" situation, *everyone* was acting strangely. Men and women alike. There was little chance that I'd be able to discern the difference, so I finally gave up and tried to enjoy our win.

I guess I wasn't the only one having a problem with this, because the party fizzled out quickly. I don't know about anyone else, but all I wanted to do was go to bed.

Chapter Seven

Saturday, October 4

As I was getting ready for work, my phone rang. It was Rick.

"Hey Rick! What's up?" I asked.

"Hey, Sis! I'm calling about the photos I took at the tournament finals. You said it was definitely a man that was in the women's locker rooms with you, right? So in my attempt to get photos of every single male at the tournament, I ended up with nearly a thousand photos," Rick said. "There had to be close to five hundred people at the tournament."

"Oh, my. That's a lot," I said, taking a much-needed sip of my morning coffee.

"It is," he agreed. "So, I ran the photos through some AI software that I use for my bird watching. It used things like body type, clothing, facial features, height, and where people were sitting, to match up photos of the same person."

"Cool! Did it work?" I asked.

"Yep, it did. It came up with approximately one hundred potentially distinct males. Of those, twenty-three were children, based on their size and other factors. That left just over seventy-five adult males that were of interest."

"Huh. I would have expected more," I said. "Were you able to identify any of them?"

"Yes, well, our dad was an easy one." We both laughed.

"Coach Masayuki was another. His tennis outfit and floppy hat were pretty unique."

"Oh yes, his hat! It looks silly, but keeps the sun off his face and neck when he's not actually playing tennis," I said. "And I wouldn't exactly call Dad and Coach 'males of interest'," I said.

"True," Rick agreed. "Then there were a few others. Steve was easily identifiable, as he was always at Sharon's side or with his daughter. He also had two small dogs with him. He did leave early though."

"This is starting to sound like a bust," I said, disappointment evident in my voice.

"There was one interesting item of note," Rick said. "I saw Brandon. And he wasn't picketing. He almost seemed like he was trying to disguise himself. Hat. Sunglasses. Lurking behind pillars and things."

"Oh! Well, that is interesting. Could you tell why he was there? Was he with someone?"

"Not that I could see. I don't know. I just think it was strange," Rick said. "Oh, I did see Mr. Piatt, our old high school history teacher!"

"Mr. Piatt! Wow. I don't think I've ever seen him at the courts," I said. "Well, thanks for doing this, Rick. Can you send me a link to the photos so I can look at them later? I need to get to work."

"You got it, Sis. Have a great day at work! Give Clover a kiss for me. Love you, Sis."

"Love you back!" I said.

~

ONCE AT WORK, CLOVER SETTLED DOWN ON HER WINDOW perch, and I whipped out my computer tablet so I could take a look at the photos Rick had sent over. I was thankful he had pared it down to only seventy or so men!

Brandon was interesting, as Rick had said. He spent a lot of time near the tournament players, but I couldn't tell what he was doing. I put him under my mental "persons of interest" list.

And, Steve was indeed there with his dogs. At one point it seemed that he had a conversation with Brandon, but it must have been a short one, because there were only three photos capturing their encounter. Steve and the dogs weren't in any more photos after that. Hmm. Curious.

There was a guy that I thought I recognized from one of the shops in town. Maybe he worked at one of the eateries? Or perhaps the pet store? I couldn't quite place him.

I recognized a guy that was dating Tracy, my left-handed competitor. But he was too skinny to have been the guy that knocked me over in the locker room.

The rest were men like Henry from the antique shop and Juste from the bakery, or people I just didn't know.

Rats. Well, this was indeed a bust. Maybe I'd print a few of the photos so I could look at them again later with fresh eyes.

As I stuck the tablet back in the drawer, the doors chimed and to my complete and happy surprise, Jeremy walked into my shop!

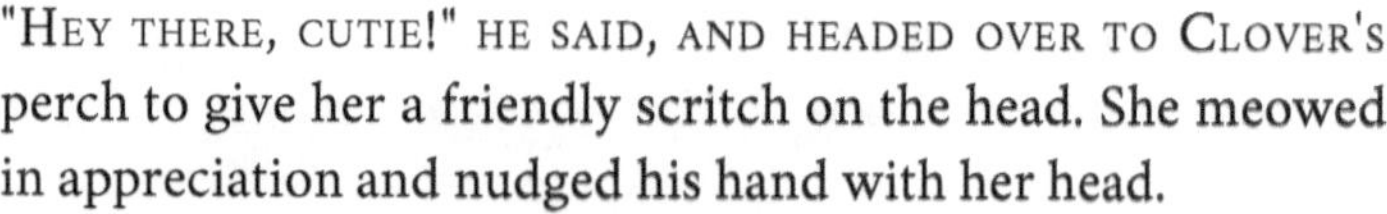

"HEY THERE, CUTIE!" HE SAID, AND HEADED OVER TO CLOVER'S perch to give her a friendly scritch on the head. She meowed in appreciation and nudged his hand with her head.

"Were you talking to me or the cat?" I asked.

"Huh?" he asked, turning toward me.

"You said 'cutie' and I was just wondering which of us you were addressing."

Jeremy laughed. It was a lovely sound that fit his warm personality.

"You, of course," he said, giving me a big grin. He joined me at the sales counter.

"Good answer," I replied. I gave a quick look around the small shop to make sure it was still empty, then asked, "So. Anything on the racket?"

"I missed you, too," he said.

I blushed. "Oh, gosh, I'm sorry. That was rude. It's just been on my mind a lot, as you can imagine," I said.

"I get it," he said. "I just wouldn't want to think that you're only interested in me for my access to information."

I could tell that though he was trying to make light of it, it was a real concern for him.

I shook my head emphatically. "Absolutely not. In fact, don't tell me anything. You're right. It's none of my business." In order to give him time to think about it, I tried to look busy behind the counter, moving papers around and straightening up the stapler and tape dispensers.

He studied me for a few moments, then said, "No, I can't believe that of you. And besides, the way I see it, you have every right to know. After all, you single-handedly found both the body and the murder weapon."

"To be fair, it was actually *you* that found the murder weapon," I said with a wink.

"Don't remind me!" he said, rolling his eyes. "That being said, I guess we now know what those mysterious marks were on his body."

"Oh, right!" I said, as it dawned on me. "I thought that pattern looked familiar. It was from the stitching that attaches the strings to the tennis racket's frame."

"Yup."

"Great! So then, what's the news on the racket?" I asked.

"As you might expect," Jeremy said, "a tennis racket isn't the best object to get good fingerprints from. The way a racket is used tends to overlay and smear any prints. That being said, we did get two fairly clear prints, and what looks like a palm print."

"That's great!" I said.

"Don't get too excited yet," he said. "Prints don't help if you have nothing to compare them to. The prints weren't in any of the usual databases, like the Automated Fingerprint Identification System, or 'AFIS' for short."

"Why not?" I asked.

"Well, the databases are for fingerprints taken from arrests, or from teachers, or permits to carry a concealed weapon, law enforcement... that kinda thing. If prints are from someone whose fingerprints have no reason to be in any of these databases, then we have to go about getting a match some other way."

"What do you mean?" I asked.

"Well, we need something to compare them to. But we can't exactly print the entire city. We don't have probable cause for that."

"Probable cause?"

"Yes," he said. "We need a valid reason to invade people's privacy."

"And murder isn't enough?" I asked, aghast.

"It is, but printing the hundreds of people that were at the tournament is no small task."

"Well, what about DNA then?" I asked.

"DNA has been collected, but it can take weeks to get results. This isn't TV. Besides, we're a small town so we have to send it out to a larger lab for analysis."

I shook my head in dismay, as I thought about all of this for a moment.

"We also found *two* separate sets of footprints in or around the blood on the floor of the locker room."

"Two? Besides the killer, who would have left footprints in the blood?"

"We're not sure. One set was small. Possibly female. The second set looked to be about a size ten shoe. So probably male."

"Wow. I guess you can't do much with that until you have some suspects, right? You can't go searching everyone's shoe closets."

"Can you imagine?" Jeremy said with a laugh. "And just one more thing..." Jeremy said, holding up his index finger. "Turns out that the hairs they found in the blood at Matteo's crime scene are not human, and they're not synthetic. Most likely, they're from an animal. If so, the lab will be able to tell us what type of animal they're from. We were also able to confirm that it was the same type of hair that was stuck in the blood on the racket we found. Just like you thought." He smiled at me. "Impressive crime scene skills you have there."

"Well, thank you," I said, blushing with pleasure. "Will those results take less time than the DNA?" I asked.

Before he could answer, Denise Christensen entered my store!

"Denise!" I said in surprise. "How nice to see you! Glad to see you found a racket in time for the tournament. That was lucky. You played great, by the way."

She smiled and waved her hand dismissively. "Hardly. That racket *sucked*. But thanks anyway." She meandered slowly over to the display of tennis rackets.

I joined her there, while Jeremy made himself look busy, while still staying close enough to eavesdrop on us.

"What's your most expensive racket?" Denise asked, running her finger over a few of the options.

"Uh, you mean our best racket?" I asked.

"Same thing, right?" she asked.

"Okay, well, not necessarily. We have the Head line. They make excellent rackets," I said. "But Wilson makes some great rackets, too. They're all in the two to three-hundred-dollar range at the high end."

Denise picked up a few and carefully swung them around the shop a bit.

"I'll take this one," she said, holding up a three-hundred-dollar Head racket.

"Okay, great. Let's just make sure you have the right grip for the size of your hand."

We spent a few minutes trying a few grip sizes before settling on one for her.

"Any string preference?" I asked.

"Not really," she said. "Oh! And I also need a new gear bag. Mine had all this gross brown stuff all over it. I tossed it into one of the dumpsters." As she talked, she grabbed a few other items off the shelves.

What? She threw away her bag? The one with the blood on it? I widened my eyes at Jeremy while Denise wasn't looking.

Trying hard to sound casual, I rang up her purchases and asked, "So, that's too bad. Many of the more expensive leather bags," which I knew hers to be, "can be cleaned professionally. Where'd you toss it?" I looked up at her with what I hoped was a "really don't care that much" attitude.

"The tennis club, after the tournament. But I shoulda just burned it. Eew!" she said.

"Ha ha!" I tried to make my laugh sound convincing. I held up a tennis bag for her approval and she nodded.

I placed her purchases in the new tennis bag and handed it to her. "You're all set!" I said, and gave her a big smile. "See ya on the courts!"

She waved goodbye and left the store.

I took care of a few more customers that had wandered in, then Jeremy and I were alone again. I debated telling Jeremy about my plans to go dumpster diving after work for the bag, but thought better of it. He'd probably just tell me not to go, which was not what I wanted to hear right now. Besides, what if I was wrong and it wasn't blood, but instead just a bunch of brown stains?

Clover took this moment to hop onto the sales counter for some attention. It was the perfect distraction. We both gave her some love, then Jeremy said he needed to get back to work.

~

I closed up shop and figured I'd need to drop Clover at home with some food and water. Couldn't very well take a cat dumpster diving!

As I was parking the car, I saw Mrs. Chan in her garage with the door open. She didn't drive, so she had it decorated with fake grass and bamboo plants. Very cozy!

I carried Clover over to say hello and saw that she was doing Tai Chi. I was mesmerized by her slow, steady movements.

Without opening her eyes, she said, "Hello, Madeline!"

This surprised me a bit, but I replied with, "Hello, Mrs. Chan! Hope you're having a lovely day!"

At this, she opened one eye and smiled at me. "Thank you, dear. You, too." Closing her eye again, she continued with her graceful, flowing motions.

I headed back into our garage, and took Clover out of her carrier so she could run up the stairs. As I followed her, I asked, "Do you think Mrs. Chan would give me some Tai Chi lessons?"

"Meow," Clover said, heading for her water bowl.

"You're right. I'll ask next time I see her."

I fed Clover, then changed into some old black jeans, a throw-away t-shirt, and a light-weight jacket.

"It will just be a quick in and out," I told Clover.

"Meow," she said skeptically.

After dark, I drove to the tennis club and parked at the far corner of the lot where my car wouldn't be easily seen. It's not the most stealth vehicle, thanks to its bright color and my shop's car magnets on the sides. But even if I removed them, it wouldn't help much. My car stood out. So best to make this quick.

I crouched-jogged over to the unlocked, semi-enclosed structure which housed the dumpster bins. I fervently hoped that the trash hadn't been picked up yet.

I pulled open the gate-like door and was hit by a strong smell of rotten food. *Eew.* Why did the club have to serve food? I would have preferred some nice, clean trash composed primarily of water bottles and protein bar wrappers. Instead, it smelled like rotten fish.

The enclosure contained two large bins, each with heavy plastic tops. I winced as the first one swung back and hit the cinder block wall with a loud *clang.*

Occasionally, being tall came in handy. I easily peered over the top and into the smelly abyss. Well, there was no getting around it. I had to get in.

Years of tennis had made me strong. I easily hoisted myself up and over the edge and landed with a *squish* that released a fresh blast of putrid air. I should've thought to wear a mask. I rummaged around for a bit, but didn't see a tennis bag. One bin down, one to go.

I had just jumped out of the first dumpster when I saw what looked like a ghostly light suspended in the dark headed my way.

Rats! I quickly hopped into the second bin. Thankfully, it

didn't take long before I found the bag. Unfortunately, it was under a broken bag of seafood remains. I felt a sudden need to toss my cookies.

The light had made its way to my hiding place in the bin. Now I had to make a decision. Either I could hide among rotten seafood, or come up with a good excuse as to why I was trespassing on club property after hours.

My gag reflex won out and I stood up with my hands in the air. One hand was holding my prize - a wet, smelly tennis bag.

"Who's there?" asked the person with the flashlight.

"Hi! My name is Madeline. I'm a tennis player here at the club. I, uh - my mom accidentally threw away my favorite tennis bag without telling me. I just had to come back for it before the trash got taken to the dump."

"You're trespassing. We're closed."

"Um, yes. I know. I'm sorry. But can I please get out of this bin? It really stinks in here." I smiled and tried to block the light with my free hand.

"I'd rather you stay there until the police arrive."

"Police?" Oh, this had really gone sideways. "For getting my own bag out of the trash?" I tried to sound reasonable, but now I was panicking.

Before we could argue further, we saw the flashing lights of a patrol car. A female officer got out and trained her flashlight on me, other hand casually resting on her holster. She asked me to please get out of the bin. Which I gladly did.

"Name?" the officer asked me.

I sighed. "Madeline Quinn." I lowered my head in shame.

"Quinn?" she asked. "As in Police Chief Quinn?"

"Yes," I said.

The person who had first apprehended me gasped. Now that lights weren't shining in my eyes, I could finally see him.

He couldn't have been much older than me, though his security uniform made him look more mature.

I turned my attention back to the officer. "Please don't tell my sister. She'll have my head. I just wanted this bag. Uh, my bag. Got thrown away. It's my favorite..." I trailed off lamely.

"Alright," she said, with a heavy sigh. It seemed like neither of us were terribly interested in me being arrested (so much paperwork!). "Just make sure you go straight home." She turned to the club security guard. "You okay with this?"

"Uh, yeah, I guess. I mean, sure. If you say so," he said.

I breathed a sigh of relief. "Thank you. Both of you." I tried to look as contrite as possible. They both gave weary nods.

The law enforcement folk went back to their nights, and I thanked my lucky stars as I drove home with the bag. I hoped it would be worth it.

~

I GOT HOME WITH MY SMELLY EVIDENCE AND IMMEDIATELY threw it out onto my balcony. Even Clover ran from me when I brought it through the kitchen. I couldn't leave it there overnight, though. At least not without first trying to preserve whatever evidence wasn't already contaminated by the trash it had been rotting in all day.

I knew from my casual studies of forensics and listening to Annabelle talk about evidence, that I had to keep it in a paper bag, or some other breathable container. If you put potentially biological evidence in a plastic bag, you get a virtual Petri dish of bacteria, effectively ruining any DNA or blood evidence.

I rummaged around in my closet until I found a paper bag large enough to hold the tennis bag.

I put the tennis bag in the paper bag and stapled the top

closed. Then I took it down to the garage to protect it from the elements. I sat the bag on top of my car.

The next order of business was to take a long, hot shower. I went into my bathroom and stripped out of my clothes, tossing them into the tub. I would have to decide if they were worth keeping. Or maybe burning.

Clover sat in the doorway, sitting primly with her tail wrapped around herself. She reminded me of an Egyptian cat statue when she sat like that. It made me smile. And it also reminded me that I still had to pick up my cat statue from Henry's antique shop! Dang it.

Normally, Clover would be in the bathroom with me, getting under foot, as cats do. But my guess is the smell of my clothes kept her at bay.

I stepped into the shower, with the water as hot as I could stand it, and scrubbed down. Then I scrubbed down again. My coconut-water body gel helped clear my sinuses of the smell that seemed to cling to my nose hairs. Maybe a sinus rinse after the shower was also in order.

Finally, I dried off and put on some comfy pajamas. I put my clothes into a garbage bag and tossed them into my garage.

Then I made my way back upstairs to the kitchen and poured myself a glass of wine, which I desperately needed.

I sat down on the couch and was graced by the presence of Clover on my lap.

I stroked her fur, and sipped my wine, as I decided what to do with the evidence. Do I bring it to Jeremy? He was a CSI after all. His job is all about handling evidence. Or do I bring it to my sister, aka, the Chief of Police. She'd find out eventually what I'd been up to, assuming the lady cop from earlier tonight hadn't already spilled the beans.

No. I think I would have heard something by now if that

had been the case. So I had a reprieve before that hit the fan, at least. I sighed.

I suppose a third option would be dropping it off anonymously at the station, but someone would be bound to recognize me. I sighed again. Having a sister as the chief brought with it both benefits and drawbacks. Considering my nose for trouble, I'd take the benefits any day.

I decided to take the bag to Annabelle tomorrow morning. Hopefully, she wouldn't be too angry with me.

Chapter Eight

Sunday, October 5

The next morning, I called to make an appointment to see my sister, the Chief. Poor thing was working another Sunday. I had to arrange for Nikki to cover me at work, as my appointment was right in the middle of the morning.

I arrived at the station and checked in at the front desk.

"Oh, hi, Madeline! The Chief is ready to see you."

I thanked her and found my way to Annabelle's office. As expected, it looked as though she'd been living in it. Empty Chinese take-out boxes in the trash, lots of Styrofoam cups filled with varying amounts of old coffee, and a very tired-looking sister.

"Hey, Maddie," she said.

"Hey, Sis." I moved some manila folders off a chair and sat down.

"So what's this about a bag?"

Okay. So much for pleasantries. I told her the story, starting from the finals where I first saw the blood on the bag and noticed that Denise was missing her tennis racket, up to the trash-bin-fiasco night.

Her eyes got increasingly narrow as my story unfolded, until she finally just closed her eyes and put her head in her hands.

"Okay. So let me get this straight," she said, looking up at me again. "You discovered potential evidence in a murder, but rather than calling me, or 911 even, you took it upon yourself to retrieve this evidence on your own, managing to trespass on private property and potentially contaminate the bag further. Not to mention the chain of custody..."

"I don't-" I began.

Annabelle raised her hand to silence me. "Do you under-stand the potential ramifications of breaking the chain of custody? The bag could conceivably be declared inadmissible in court. You are not an officer of the law. In court, they could say you tampered with, contaminated, or even planted the evidence."

"I would never-"

"If we cannot demonstrate that you were in possession of the bag since the time you found it... Speaking of, why didn't you just hand it over to the officer that was called to the scene? Why did you let her believe the bag was yours?"

I thought about that for a moment. "I honestly have no idea. It never even occurred to me to hand it over. I was just so embarrassed at getting caught. I guess I just wanted out of there as quickly as possible."

She looked at me for a long while, as though deciding my truthfulness, then nodded. "Well, what's done is done. Hopefully it will be enough that you're my sister. Technically, because the bag was obtained illegally, it could mean any subsequent evidence we obtain as a result will be fruit of the poisonous tree."

"Poisonous tree? You mean it might be worthless?"

"We have options, but you've made things a lot harder for us," she said.

"Oh, god," I said. "I'm so sorry. Truly. I really didn't think it through. I guess I just got all caught up in it."

"I get it. I really do. But just go home now please, and stay out of trouble. Leave the detective work to the professionals."

"But doesn't this now mean that Denise is an official suspect?" I asked. "I mean, it *was* her racket that we found, right?"

"Yes, it was hers. When we processed the racket, we found her name monogrammed beneath the blood. But whether or not she is a suspect remains to be seen. Let's not get ahead of ourselves. We're still waiting on DNA and fingerprints, and we still have to process the bag."

"Right." I stood up. "Thanks for helping me out, Sis. Sorry if I made things harder on you."

She got up and gave me a hug. "It's kinda par for the course when you have a little sister."

A FEW HOURS AFTER I MET WITH ANNABELLE, I GOT TOGETHER with Rick and Lizzy to compare notes on our current list of suspects. I went to an office supply store to pick up a whiteboard, a label maker, and some lined sticky notes. By the time Rick and Lizzy had arrived, I had set out snacks and drinks, and had my board set up with our first four suspects.

"Wow, super pro job, Sis!" Rick said as he opened his Coke. He took a seat on the couch and Lizzy sat next to him.

"Yeah, run us through it, Mads!" Lizzy said.

I stood near the board. Right in the middle, I had Coach Matteo with sticky notes saying "Motives: womanizer?," "tennis money?," and "stolen student?".

"So, I've written down the reasons I think someone may have wanted to kill Coach Matteo. Let me know if you can think of any other reasons," I said. "I also have our four suspects: Coach Masayuki, Brandon the pickleball guy, our Mystery Man, and Denise."

"Is Denise really a suspect? From what you told us, it seems like Matteo was pretty beat up for it to have been a woman," Rick said. Lizzy and I both gave him a look. "What?" he asked defensively.

"You don't think a woman can do some serious damage?" Lizzy asked.

"Especially when angry?" I added, eyes narrowed.

Rick held his hands up in surrender. "Okay, okay. She's a suspect! Are you happy now?" Rick asked.

"Oh my god! That reminds me," I said. "I didn't tell you about the bloody tennis bag!" I gave them a slightly edited version of my embarrassing escapade, trying to make myself sound as slick-sleuth-like as possible. "And we now know that the racket did indeed belong to Denise. Annabelle confirmed this."

"I can't believe you went dumpster diving by yourself at night! Are you crazy? You could have gotten hurt, arrested, or worse!" Lizzy said, glaring at me.

"Maybe you're just upset that she did it without you," Rick suggested.

Lizzy rolled her eyes at him. "Whatever. Still, I guess it means that Denise definitely belongs on the board."

We all nodded in agreement. "As unlikely as it sounds," I said, "there's enough evidence that we can't eliminate her. I know it's circumstantial evidence for now. At least until they have time to process everything. It's really just a gut feeling at this point. I feel like she's involved somehow."

Rick said, "Maybe Denise has a jealous admirer that killed him?"

"Ooh! Good one," I said. Next to Denise's photo and name, I added sticky notes with "bloody tennis bag," "racket weapon," "Coach Matteo's lover?," and "jealous admirer?"

"It's good to see you have Brandon on there," Rick said, dipping a chip in the queso dip I'd bought at Trader Joe's. "I don't like that pickle guy."

Next to Brandon's name and photo, I'd written "fought with Coach Matteo."

"I don't like him either," I said. "But right now I don't have a lot on him."

"Yeah, but let's keep him up there for now," Lizzy said.

"And, as much as I hate to think about it, I feel like I have to have Coach Masayuki on here," I said. "If he really did steal Courtney from Coach Matteo, there could potentially be a lot of money there." Next to his photo and name, my notes said, "Courtney goes pro?," and "tennis money?," and "seen fighting with CM."

Rick popped a soda cracker into his mouth. "So just how much money does a tennis coach make, anyway? Should I be thinking of a career change?"

We all laughed. I shook my head. "Oh, it's not about how much money tennis coaches make, though that can be significant if you're coaching pros. It's about the money that comes from pro competitions and winning titles. For example, the coach to Venus and Serena Williams is said to have earned more than fifteen percent of their winnings. They may also sometimes get a salary. When Venus won Wimbledon in 2000, she won four hundred and thirty thousand pounds. That's a one hundred and twenty-three thousand pound paycheck for her coach."

Rick whistled. "Not bad."

"And just think... since that time, Venus has raked in tens of millions of dollars in prize money." I said. Rick whistled again.

"But there's no guarantee that Courtney is going to be anywhere near that good," Lizzy pointed out.

"There's a good chance she will, based on what I've seen," I said. "And with the right coach..."

"I just find it so hard to imagine Coach Masayuki wanting to hurt anyone, let alone kill them," Lizzy said.

"It could have been an accident," Rick said. "Or a heat-of-the-moment kinda thing."

"Then if that's the case," Lizzy said, "my money is on Brandon."

We all nodded in agreement.

"So what about our mystery man from the locker room? What was his motive?" Rick asked.

"He has to have been after the racket. But how he knew it was in the women's locker room, I don't know," I said. "I also think we need to figure out where Brandon was during the time frame of Coach Matteo's death. Means and motive mean nothing if he didn't have the opportunity to commit the murder."

"I'll see if I can find out," Rick said. "Maybe he'll talk to me. Man to man."

"Well, please be careful," Lizzy said. "I don't want you ticking off a potential killer."

Rick smiled. "Worried about me, Liz?"

"Of course I am," she said. "You're my best friend's brother."

I studied her face. Is that really all it was? I wasn't convinced, but didn't have time to dwell on it now.

"I'll try to get to Courtney," Lizzy said, changing the subject. "She's probably still wary of talking to you, Mads."

"Good plan," I said. "Then I'll talk to Denise. But I'm coming with both of you when you talk to Brandon and Courtney!"

I got immediate protests from Lizzy and Rick.

"No!" Rick said. "That will mess up the whole 'bro to bro' thing."

"And if you're there, Courtney won't talk to me!" Lizzy said.

I had already started shaking my head. "No, no, no," I said. "I'm not going to do the interviews with you. I'm just going to be nearby so I can hear what they say and see how they behave. You'll never know I'm there, I swear."

Lizzy and Rick looked dubious, but in the end, I won them over.

Chapter Nine

Wednesday, October 8

A few days later, Lizzy arranged to run into Courtney around the time of her tennis lesson with Coach Masayuki. The problem was, there weren't a lot of places for me to eavesdrop without being seen.

We discussed the possibilities, and decided that she would hang out in the women's locker room near the sinks until Courtney came in.

I was able to hide around the corner near the lockers. If anyone had come in, I could pretend to be getting dressed for tennis.

The good news was that Lizzy's plan worked like a charm. Courtney did come in and they did start up a conversation. Unfortunately, that conversation didn't take long enough for my hiding place to ever become a problem.

"Hey Courtney," Lizzy said, pretending to dry her hands on a small, rolled-up hand towel.

Courtney stopped short, already suspicious. "Lizzy."

"I know Coach Masayuki won't let you talk to Mads, but maybe you can talk to me?" she asked.

"There's really nothing to say, Lizzy. I didn't see anything. I don't know anything. If I did, I'd tell someone about what I knew, no matter what Coach said. But I don't. You just have to believe me."

"Yeah, okay. I understand," Lizzy said.

"Good." With that, Courtney left the locker rooms without using the facilities.

After a few moments, I left my hiding place.

"Well," I said, "it was worth a try."

"I'm sorry," Lizzy said. "Hopefully Rick will get Brandon to talk." She looked down at her hands, dejected.

I put a gentle hand on her shoulder. "Hey, you tried. And besides, Courtney is a quiet, young girl. Brandon is a loud-mouthed jerk. Rick has the easier assignment by far."

"True," Lizzy said, looking back up at me with a small smile.

"Maybe we should have switched you two up. Had you talk to Brandon and Rick to Courtney," I said, half-jokingly. At the look of horror on Lizzy's face, I laughed. "Just kidding! Don't worry about it. We can always try again."

LATER THAT EVENING, RICK ARRANGED TO "RUN INTO" Brandon at Sycamore Cove's local watering hole, The Alibi.

"I've seen him here more than a few times," Rick said to me before we went in. "So I knew he'd show up sooner or later. That's his car." Rick nodded toward a VW Bug that looked like it had seen better days. It was mostly yellow, with a lot of rust spots and old crusty rims.

Approaching The Alibi, we peeked through the windows and saw that Brandon was sitting at the bar, his back toward the front door. However, the walls behind the bar were covered in mirrors, so we couldn't easily sneak in through the front.

Rick turned to me. "Okay, look. I'll come in the front and head straight for him. You go in through the back while I have him distracted."

"Got it," I said. I moved away from the windows and headed around to the back door. When I saw Rick approach the bar, I entered the room in time to hear him greet Brandon. I sat in a quiet corner, close enough to hear them talk, but with a wooden pillar in their line of sight to me.

"Hey man!" Rick said loudly. "It's Brandon, right? The pickleball hero?"

Peeking around my pillar, I could see that Brandon had turned, beer in hand, to see who was talking to him. The start of a smile tugged at the side of his mouth. "Hey. Um, hero?"

Rick sat down next to Brandon and waved down the bartender. "I'd like to buy this guy's next beer! He's the hero of pickleballers everywhere! And I'll take a beer too, please." The bartender was unimpressed, but slid a fresh beer in front of Brandon, who was fully smiling now, and one in front of Rick.

"Well, I don't know about that. I just do some picketing here and there," Brandon said modestly.

"Ha! 'Some' picketing," Rick said, sipping his beer. "I see you all the time on the courts, man. You're relentless. Tireless. Dedicated."

I winced. Okay, Rick, don't oversell it.

Brandon didn't seem fazed though.

Rick took this moment to make his move. "Hey, what do you think about Coach Matteo's murder. You must have known him, right? Crazy stuff."

Brandon's face got dark, and he glared down at his beer. "Yeah, I know him. Over-rated Italian playboy."

"Oh," Rick said. "Well, I remember seeing you at the tournament. I thought maybe you'd seen something that would help with the case."

"What are you? A cop?" Brandon asked, eyes narrowed in suspicion. "I left when everyone else did, man." He stood up and pushed his half-full beer back toward the bartender. "You can keep your free beer, man. Leave me alone." With that, Brandon stormed out of the bar.

A few patrons who had been watching curiously as things got louder, now turned back to their food and drink, interest lost.

Rick took his beer, headed toward my table, and sat down. "Well, that was a bust. Sorry, Sis."

"That's okay," I said, reaching over to pat his hand in consolation. "Let me buy you dinner for your efforts."

This perked up his mood. We smiled at each other and waved down a waitress.

Chapter Ten

Saturday, October 11

The day of Matteo Amato's funeral had arrived. I don't like funerals, for obvious reasons. But I wanted to pay my respects, and it would be a good opportunity to observe anyone who may have had a problem with the coach.

His parents had flown in from Italy. He may not have yet established a family of his own, but his whole adult life had been spent in the United States, so they decided not to bring his body back to Italy with them.

Lizzy and I drove together with her parents. My family would meet us there, as they were coming from various other engagements. I don't think my sister had left the police station since Coach Matteo's murder, except to go to our family dinner. We don't get a lot of murders in our small, cozy town. She was under a lot of pressure to solve it. And I was going to help, and try not to make things harder for her in the process.

Lizzy and I walked in together and looked around for where to start. I've always found funerals challenging. After you pay your respects and have a bite to eat, you're left with nothing appropriate to talk about with a bunch of grieving people. It just feels wrong to laugh or smile at anything.

We gave our deepest condolences to the parents, who spoke English fairly well. Then with a few others we exchanged shock and sadness at his murder.

We then noticed Denise sitting on a couch, crying heavily. She was surrounded by a few girlfriends from tennis. One of the girls broke away from the pack and I approached her.

"Hey," I said. "Is Denise okay? I didn't realize she and Coach Matteo were that close."

"Really?" She looked me up and down incredulously. "They were a total couple. I'm surprised you missed it. Aren't you supposed to be like a wannabe sleuth or something?" She scoffed, then stalked away, leaving me shell-shocked.

Lizzy came up to me and whispered, "Are you okay? What did she say to you?"

I realized my mouth had been hanging open, so I closed it. I turned to her. "I don't know what shocks me more: that Denise and Coach really were an item, or that I seem to have a reputation for being some kind of novice crime solver."

Lizzy raised an eyebrow at me. "Seriously? You have kinda gotten involved in solving more than a few crimes since you graduated high school. In fact, I seem to recall one as far back as eleventh grade. Do you remember? You found the body of the janitor in-"

I held up a hand to stop her. "Yes, yes. How can I forget?"

I looked around the room and noticed more than one pretty young woman crying. Hmm. I elbowed Lizzy. "Seems he's brought more than a few women to tears." By my count, at least five more. I slowly wandered toward another group, followed closely by Lizzy.

"He was so good to me. He just really seemed to *understand* me, you know?" The girls sitting around comforting Denise all nodded knowingly.

Lizzy and I looked at each other. She raised another eyebrow. Before we could talk more about it, Coach Masayuki strolled through the front door. I'd only ever seen him at the tennis courts in his shorts and floppy hat, so I was floored to see him in a tasteful dark blue suit. I'm no fashionista, but I know wealth when I see it. I peeked out the front door before he'd closed it behind him to see a stunning red and black sports car parked in the driveway. It had a high spoiler and said "GT3 RS" on the side of the door. Now *that* was an expensive car.

"Woah," I said. Lizzy looked at me questioningly. "He's driving a very expensive Porsche," I whispered. "Like, you-could-buy-a-house-for-that, expensive." Her eyebrows raised in surprise.

The coach had a large platter of sushi in his hands. He looked around the room, then asked, "Anyone know where the food goes?"

I waved for his attention. "Yes, I'll take you to the kitchen," I said. He followed me, and Lizzy trailed behind him.

He set the platter on the kitchen counter and we could see that he had probably fifty pieces of sushi with him. Something about it didn't look store bought. Apparently, Lizzy thought the same thing.

"Wow!" Lizzy said. "You made all that sushi yourself?"

He smiled proudly. "Yes, it's a hobby of mine. If not eaten right away, it really should be kept chilled, but maybe it will go quickly."

"I'm happy to help with that!" I said enthusiastically. I just love sushi and all things seafood since I first tried escargot at the tender young age of nine.

"Please!" he said. He pulled back the plastic wrap for me, then leaned against the counter, surveying the food others had brought.

"Don't sushi chefs use special knives for this?" Lizzy

asked. "The slices are all so uniform. So precise," she said, filling a plate for herself.

Masayuki looked at her appreciatively. "Yes, thank you for noticing! I spent many years of my life working my way up through the craft."

"How did you end up a tennis coach instead of a sushi chef at some high-end Japanese restaurant?" I asked.

He shifted uncomfortably. "Let's just say that's a long story for another time."

Well, dang. Now I felt bad for asking.

Before I could make things worse, he said, "I still find the way of sushi pleasing. Just to be next to the board for a few hours a week soothes my soul. I hope you enjoy it!" With that, he walked out of the kitchen, leaving us to our delicious sushi.

My brow furrowed. "Did he seem sad about not being a sushi chef to you?"

"Yeah," Lizzy said, popping a spicy tuna roll into her mouth. "Wonder what really happened?"

"Me, too," I said. "Ah, well. We should probably go mingle some more before we eat this entire platter ourselves!"

We left the kitchen and made a few more rounds of the room, got a few more finger foods and wine, then found a centrally located place where we could observe almost everyone at the gathering. It worked out even better than I had hoped. People would walk slowly by us, absorbed in their conversations. We got to hear all kinds of interesting things.

At one point, Sharon and her husband Steve walked by. They didn't even see us.

"Well, of course he looks like a million bucks," Sharon said. "Masayuki Noguchi is a trust fund baby, after all. Oh yes. His parents died in a plane crash. Left him a business and millions of dollars. Why he wants to spend his time teaching tennis to a bunch of-" Before I could hear the rest, they walked out of earshot.

I immediately removed a small notebook from my purse and jotted this new information down. A few minutes later, Sharon and Steve were making their way back toward us when Steve stopped short, putting his arm out to stop Sharon next to him. The look on his face was unbridled anger.

"What the-" I started to whisper to Lizzy. Then I saw who he was looking at. It was Brandon, who was headed their way with a purposeful stride and a sneer on his face. The next thing I knew, as he walked past, Brandon clipped Steve in the shoulder hard enough to knock him off balance.

I thought this was going to accelerate into a full-blown fight when Sharon put a calming hand on her husband's shoulder, whispering something in his ear.

Brandon turned back toward them and made a mock bow. "My apologies to you and your lovely wife." He winked at Sharon and walked away. Steve and Sharon went the other direction.

"What the heck was that all about?" Lizzy whispered.

"I have no idea, but it sure was interesting." I jotted notes on the altercation in my notebook.

After sitting with Lizzy for a few more quiet minutes, I finally got up the courage to talk to Coach Masayuki. He'd been rather adamant about not wanting to talk to me at the courts, but maybe our friendly conversation about sushi would shift things in my favor.

I found him making the rounds of mourners and stopped him with a gentle hand on his arm. "Coach?" I asked.

He didn't seem too happy to see me again, but he didn't tell me to go away. I took that as my opening.

"There's a rumor going around that you stole Courtney from Coach Matteo for the potential money she'll make once she goes pro. Maybe he confronted you about it, and you killed him? I'm sure it was an accident. Heat of the moment kinda thing."

He couldn't have looked more shocked than if I'd told him the world was ending in the next five minutes. So shocked, in fact, that he was speechless for a moment.

"Wait. What?! Is that why you've been wanting to talk to me? To accuse me of stealing a client and murdering the man I allegedly stole from?" He crossed his arms across his chest and stared down at me. "Besides, I have plenty of money. I don't need to steal anyone's student."

"Uh, well..." I stuttered. "Maybe you've already spent it all?" I don't know what response I'd been expecting, but it wasn't that. Maybe a heart-felt confession?

"And this is the venue you choose for your assault on my character?"

Actually, he had a point. In fact, I was starting to feel pretty silly. My face turned as red as my hair. Which, with my pale complexion, was quite the sight.

Lizzy suddenly appeared by my side. "When you wouldn't talk to her, what did you expect her to think?"

He turned his cold gaze in her direction. "Not that I had *killed* someone. Just that my life was none of her business."

Lizzy nodded. "That's fair."

I looked at her, betrayed. She shrugged. "What?"

Looking back at Coach Masayuki, I said, "You and Coach Matteo had a very public argument. And he had a black eye and a broken rib. Sounds like things got pretty physical to me. Maybe came to blows?" I stared boldly up at him.

The ghost of some emotion crossed his face. He heaved a heavy sigh. "All right. Look. I probably gave him the broken rib, but that's it. I don't like to speak ill of the dead, but the man is - was - a womanizer. Some of those women were my students. I was just trying to... put a damper on his libido."

Lizzy and I looked at each other sadly. It was hard to hear that Coach Matteo really was a womanizer. That it wasn't just gossip.

"You're the one that gave him a broken rib? But not the black eye?"

"Yes. And I was ashamed of it. That's the real reason I didn't want to talk to you. It was a stupid and immature thing to do. I was angry. But when I left him curled up in a ball on the ground, he was alive. You might want to start looking for an angry boyfriend or husband. Good day."

With that, he dropped his arms, spun on his heel, and walked quickly away.

I felt the eyes of more than a few people on me, so I grabbed Lizzy's arm and pulled her into the relatively empty kitchen. She jumped on me as soon as we were – sort of – alone.

"And just what did you think would happen just now?" Lizzy asked with exasperation. "That he'd break down crying and admit his guilt to everyone at a funeral?"

I shrugged. "I don't know. No? Maybe? I mean, it always works for Hannah Swensen. You could have at least backed me up in there. Maybe be good cop to my bad cop?"

Lizzy gaped at me. "I'm sorry... Did you say Hannah... Are you referring to Hannah Swensen from Hallmark's 'Murder, She Baked' series? Are you serious? Mads, this is real life, not television. And you're not a cop."

I tried to look chastised, but I couldn't stop thinking about next steps. I probably only had time for one more move before the funeral started winding down. Just then, my brother Rick walked into the kitchen.

"Rick!" I said.

"Maddie! Do you know where the bathrooms are?"

"Sorry, no." An idea came to me. "Hey! Do you know if Brandon is still here?"

"Brandon? Yeah, he's here. Seems everyone is, whether friend or foe."

"Great. Can the bathroom wait? Take me to where you last saw him." I grabbed my brother's arm and dragged him out to the living room.

"Uh, I think I saw him in this media room with the big screen TV. Yep. There he is." Rick pointed to Brandon and a few other folks I knew to be pickleball players.

I walked up to them and said, "Hey, Brandon. Didn't expect to see you here today."

He looked at me without a spark of recognition.

"Madeline," I said. "I talked to you the other day while you were-"

"Oh, yeah. You." He gave me a look of annoyance. "And *you* again," he said, spotting Rick standing behind me.

Yup. He recognized me, alright.

One of the female pickleballers said, "And why wouldn't we be here? We're all racket players, after all."

"Oh, yeah. I guess so." Hmm. I should start selling pickleball gear in my shop.

"So," I said. "I had a few more questions for you about Coach Matteo."

"I told you already. Nothing happened," he said. "We had words. I left."

"You said you never touched him, but I'm told he had a broken rib and black eye." I didn't need to let him know that I knew the broken rib happened earlier in the day, and that it was Coach Masayuki that had given it to him.

"Ha! A guy like that? Hit me? I'd like to see him try. I gave him a good smack in the eye, but it was his own fault, trying to grab my picketing sign. But that's it. I. Did. Not. Kill. Him. And hey, I'm not the only one Coach Matteo had been arguing with. Maybe you should stop pestering me, and go bark up *that* tree, lady." With that, he turned back to his friends without giving me another thought.

Lady? Bark? Wow, that was rude on so many levels, I was speechless. Which doesn't happen to me all that often.

"Sorry to bother you," Rick said, taking my arm to pull me away.

"Whatever," Brandon said, dismissing us with a wave of the back of his hand.

Well, that was another bust. Two suspects down, but no confession.

"Come on, Rick. Let's grab Lizzy and get out of here," I said.

Chapter Eleven

Sunday, October 12

It was time to pay a visit to Denise. But I couldn't go there empty-handed, so I headed for Lizzy's candle bar and shop to make a one-of-a-kind candle for her as a gift.

The candle shop had a fantastic location right on the harbor. I took a deep breath of ocean air, then opened the front door to Wicked Wicks, Lizzy's candle shop. A bell quietly chimed my arrival.

Lizzy, who was behind the candle bar, called out her hello.

"Mads! What a pleasant surprise!"

One of the nice things about owning a retail store is that you can start late. It was already ten in the morning, but she was just opening up the shop. I helped her set up the candle bar with the trays the guests would use to collect the items they'd need to create a candle from scratch. On each tray, we put a paper place mat which held instructions on how to do it and suggestions for various popular scent combinations like vanilla, sandalwood, and citrus scents.

"So what are you doing here?" she asked.

I started a slow walk down the ever-changing wall of scented oils. I ran my finger over the labels: vanilla bean, cinnamon, seagrass, coconut. The choices seemed endless.

"I'm going to visit Denise today," I said. "I want to bring her a custom candle as a sort of ice breaker slash sorry your boyfriend died kinda thing. Got any scent combos that say that?"

We both gave a rather uncomfortable laugh.

"Hmm..." she said, rubbing her chin in thought. "Why don't you grab the container you want and a wick, and I'll pick out some possibilities."

I sat on one of the high stools at the candle bar and set my tray in front of me. I had chosen a wooden wick for my candles, which crackles like a fireplace, and a classic, timeless jar with a frosted thick glass base.

Lizzy came over with a small basket filled with about five or six bottles of fragrance oils.

"Okay," she said, setting the bottles on the counter as she called out the scents. "I've got some lavender, chamomile, cedar wood, peppermint, eucalyptus, and vanilla bean."

I sniffed a few of the choices, then went with the lavender and vanilla. I also asked her for a honey scent. I felt calm just thinking about it!

"I need enough to make two. I'm making one for myself as well," I said.

"Great idea!" she replied.

At Lizzy's direction, I centered my wick, held in place with a special holder, then poured my unique blend of scents and creamy soy wax into my containers. While I worked, we chatted about the Sycamore Cove Harvest Festival that was coming up in October.

"So, Lizzy," I said. "What are you planning for your booth at the Harvest Festival?"

"Oh! I can't wait," Lizzy said. "I will have my usual selection of fall candles of course: Christmas Peppermint, Pine Tree, Cinnamon Birch, and of course Holiday Sugar Cookie. Then I'll have some tapered candles that the kids can dip into colorful wax, making their own candles. They make great Christmas gifts."

"That sounds fantastic!" I said, finishing up my candles. "I hope you'll get some help with your booth, so we can hang out together."

"Of course!" Lizzy said, carefully moving my newly poured candles to a shelf to cool. "Okay, girl. You know the drill. It's gonna take about ninety minutes for these to cool enough for you to take them home with you, so why don't you head over to Kay's Koffee Shop and get us some cappuccinos and fresh baked goods! I want a chocolate croissant, please!"

"Coming right up," I said with a smile. I left the candle shop and made the short walk past some of the harbor shops until I came to Kay's Koffee. Her door was propped open with one of those a-frame tent signs which listed the day's specials.

I got into line and waited my turn to get my goodies. When I got to the register, I saw Kay herself.

"Hey, Mads!" Kay said with a big smile. "What brings you to the harbor?"

"Oh, just stopped by Lizzy's to make a candle for Denise as a sort of condolence gift. I have to wait for her candle to cool, so I thought we'd snack on some goodies in the meantime."

"I think that's a great idea, of course," Kay said with a laugh as she rang me up. "Why does Denise need a condolence candle? Is everything okay with her?"

"Well, it's my understanding that she and Matteo Amato were seeing each other," I said. "You know, the tennis coach that was just murdered?"

She grimaced. "Yeah, I know of him." Kay looked around at the rather small crowd in her shop, nodded to her assistant, then said to me, "Hey. Let's sit down for a quick minute."

Kay and I moved to a table for two that was close to the register in case she was needed. "I thought Denise was seeing some other guy," Kay said, her brows crinkled in thought. "Brian? Braydon?"

My jaw dropped. It had been doing that a lot lately. "Wait! Are you talking about Brandon? The annoying pickleballer?"

She snapped her fingers. "Brandon! Yep. That's it."

I shook my head in disbelief. I couldn't wait to get back to Lizzy with this crazy news! But first, I had to ask, "Kay, are you going to have a booth at the Harvest Festival?"

"I wouldn't miss it!" she said. "In fact, I'm going to have two locations. One will be a coffee cart with the usual cookies and hot chocolate and stuff, and then an actual booth where I'll sell our special Kay's Koffee bags. I plan to have a few wonderful winter-themed blends." She smiled with excitement.

"That sounds amazing," I said. "I can't wait!" I gave her a quick hug, a large cash tip, and gathered my loot. "Thanks, Kay. You're the best!" I headed toward the door with a wave goodbye.

I came quickly through the front door of the candle shop, startling the customers perusing the scent selection.

I winced and said, "Sorry! Sorry." I quietly took the food to a hidden spot behind the register.

Lizzy spent about thirty minutes helping the guests start their custom candles, then finally had time for me and her coffee, which was now cold.

"You took your sweet time! Where's my food?" She asked in a whisper. "And what's got you all excited?"

"Kay says she thought Denise was seeing Brandon!"

Lizzy wrinkled her nose at this. "Really? I mean, he's a nice-looking guy, I guess. If you don't mind dating a Neanderthal."

"Hey!" I said. "Neanderthals had pretty big brains!"

She gave me a funny look. "Okay... What I mean is, he's a bit of a knuckle-dragger for my taste, but to each their own."

My enthusiasm cooled a bit. "Yeah, it does seem unlikely, I guess." I thoughtfully took a bite of my second macadamia coconut cookie. "I guess I'll find out when I take her the candle. Speaking of, can you please pack it up in a nice gift box? My candle can just be in a regular box."

Lizzy took care of that while I cleaned up our breakfast mess.

"Wish me luck!" I said, giving her a hug.

She handed me my beautiful candles and hugged me back. "Good luck! I hope the candle works its magic!"

I left her tending to her budding candle makers.

Denise and her parents lived in a very nice house in a very nice part of town. This was a girl who probably got a new BMW for her sixteenth birthday. In fact, a beautiful, light blue convertible BMW was parked in the driveway.

Bringing her a candle started to feel a bit underwhelming. But it was the only play I had, so I knocked on the front door.

Thankfully, Denise answered the door, and not one of her parents. I could tell she'd been crying recently.

"Hi, Denise. I brought you a little something to help lift your spirits." I held up the pretty little package.

"Thanks, Mads. That was thoughtful of you. Please come in." She turned sideways and gestured toward the inside of the home with a sweep of her arm.

I stepped into the foyer with some awe. The entry was large, with rounded walls and a high ceiling. In the middle of the foyer was a huge round table that held an equally huge bouquet of fresh flowers. On either side of the table was a circular staircase leading to the second floor.

"Let's go into the kitchen," Denise said. "Can I get you anything to eat?" she asked, leading me down a hallway lined with family photos.

"No thanks. I just ate," I said.

Denise was an only child, so there were a lot of photos of her: one for every birthday standing next to the same lamppost, lots of tournaments, school plays, and various sports award ceremonies. She even had some equestrian photos showing her jumping or riding horses.

We entered a large kitchen with an island, and a nook that seemed to seat about eight people. Two adorable Yorkies sat on a loveseat in the nook. French doors led from the kitchen to a pool and seating area with chaise lounges and large blue umbrellas. I was duly impressed.

"Wow," I said. "You sure do have a beautiful home. And your dogs are so well behaved. Not to mention adorable!"

"Thank you," she said. "They're really my dad's dogs, but I love them."

"Their hair is so long!" I said in wonder, as I watched one jump to the floor. The little thing couldn't have been more than eight inches tall, but its silvery-brown hair went all the way to the floor, smooth and glossy. On the very top of its head was a pink bow wrapped around a tuft of hair that stuck straight up. I chuckled at how cute it was. The other dog had a blue bow, so I was assuming one boy and one girl.

Denise opened the large, stainless-steel double-door fridge. "How about a Perrier?" she asked.

"Yes, please. That would be lovely," I said.

She grabbed two green bottles of sparkling water and we sat on the stools along one side of the island.

I slid the box with the candle over to her. "It was custom made for you, just this morning. The scents I chose are said to be calming. Seems you could use some of that in your life right about now. I hope you like it."

"I'm sure I will, thanks," she said.

I paused, trying to figure out how to say what I wanted to say, and ask what I wanted to ask. "So, I only realized at Matteo's funeral just how close the two of you were."

"Yes, well, with him being a coach and all, we had to be quiet about it," she said.

I nodded in understanding. Yeah, that was probably smart.

"You know," I said. "Someone told me you were seeing Brandon."

Her head snapped toward me. "What? Who said that?"

"Uh, well, I don't want to get anyone in trouble..."

"Well, you can tell whomever it was that they're wrong. Brandon wishes it were true. He won't leave me alone. Seems like every time I turn around, there he is," Denise said. Looks of fear and disgust seemed to battle for dominance on her face.

"Oh, my," I said. "That's concerning. Did you tell anyone about this? Seems a little stalker-y to me."

She nodded slowly. "Yes, Matteo knew. And my dad. I thought Dad was gonna kill him." Denise's hands wrapped tightly around the Perrier bottle.

"So, what now?" I asked.

"Well, since Matteo's murder," her voice caught for a

moment. She cleared her throat. "Since Matteo died, Brandon has been keeping his distance."

"That's good, I guess," I said. "But you should tell someone in law enforcement. Report it. It sounds like harassment if nothing else."

"Yeah," she sighed. "Can I open this now?" she asked, pulling the candle box toward her.

"Yes! Of course," I said. I didn't really want to change the subject, but I couldn't think of a good way to keep questioning her without it getting awkward.

She opened the box and pulled the candle out, setting it on the countertop.

"It's beautiful," she said. She brought the candle up to her nose and took a long, deep *sniff*. She sighed with contentment and a small smile played on her lips. She turned to me and the smile got bigger. "Thank you, Mads. I needed this. Thank you for being my friend."

Wow. Now I was getting all choked up. "I'm here for you any time," I said.

If Denise wasn't going to let the police know that Brandon had been stalking her, I would have to do it for her. She dismissed it as a nuisance, but he could be dangerous.

So I took it upon myself to meet with my sister later that afternoon. We sat in her office with cappuccinos and donuts from the gourmet break room. The station's break room did not serve the stereotypical sludge coffee and stale snacks. This was because my sister always swore that if she ever became chief, that they'd have the best of everything. The people here worked long, hard hours, she said. They deserved high quality sustenance while protecting and serving the people of Sycamore Cove.

While we munched our snacks, I gave her a summary of my conversation with Denise and watched her mentally process the information. Finally, she spoke.

"Did Denise say how long Brandon has been stalking her?" Annabelle asked.

"No, but my guess is it's been a while. I think that's why he keeps up with the pickleball ruse. If he were playing tennis, he wouldn't be able to time it so he's there when she is. At least not without being obvious. But with picketing, he can just "happen" to be on the same courts at the same time. Plus, he can easily look right at her while she plays."

"Creepy," Annabelle said. "Well, thanks to the black eye he gave Matteo, we can look into his background as part of our investigation, but unfortunately he has a right to picket if he wants to."

"Can you at least keep an eye on him?" I asked.

"Not officially, but I'll have our guys watch his movements," she said.

I sat back in my chair in relief at this news. "Great. That makes me feel much better."

"And thank you for letting me know about it," she said.

THAT NIGHT, I GATHERED MY SLEUTH BUDDIES AT MY HOUSE SO we could catch everyone up on the latest updates in the case. I thought it was time that Jeremy joined our little team. After all, we were practically dating. Plus, he had the inside scoop, thanks to his job.

I had a large pizza and some drinks set out on the coffee table.

"Wait. Brandon is stalking Denise?" Lizzy asked, horrified. "Did she tell someone? I mean, other than you?"

"No," I said. "So I did it for her. I told my sister."

"Thank god. There should be more that the police can do about stalkers. They can become dangerous," she said.

"That's true. Happens too often," Rick agreed.

"Oh, my god. I just had a thought," I said.

"What?" Jeremy asked.

I got up and started to pace. I stopped and turned to face everyone.

"What if Brandon killed Matteo because he was jealous?"

"That would make sense," Jeremy said. "But all we have on him right now is that he gave Matteo a black eye."

"But isn't that enough to question him?" Rick asked.

"Possibly," Jeremy said. "I'll talk to the Chief about it."

Chapter Twelve

Monday, October 13

Oh, man. I hate taking Clover to the vet. Clover hates it, too. Though, to be fair, Clover is the reason I hate vet day. It has nothing at all to do with the vet herself. Vicki Schmidt is an awesome veterinarian.

Before our vet appointment, I set out Clover's carrier. No big deal. Just a carrier! Could be we're just going to the tennis shop, right? Nope.

The day of the appointment always has me leaving an extra thirty minutes to even find her. How she finds a different hiding spot each time is beyond me. My place isn't that big. What is even more frustrating, is that as soon as we're in the exam room, Clover is right as rain. Happy as a clam. All of those odd, nonsensical similes.

"And how is Clover today?" Vicki asked.

"Happy, now that we're here," I said. "Crazy cat." Clover looked at me like she had no idea what my problem was.

After a quick check-up, a few shots, and a nail trimming, we let Clover hang out in her carrier snacking on treats while we caught up with gossip. It's a shame we only see each other once a year. We should hang out more.

"So, Maddie, you must have known the tennis coach who was killed, right?" Vicki asked.

"Yes, I did," I said. "In fact, I'm the one who found his body. It was horrible."

"Oh, my god. I'm so sorry! I had no idea!"

"How could you know? I don't think that was made public. Only the tennis insiders know - or *think* they know. My sister is just trying to protect me, most likely."

Vicki nodded. "Speaking of, do the police have any idea yet who did it?"

"No, not yet. There's a handful of suspects, but no one has been arrested yet," I said.

"Well, I hope they're caught soon. Scary having a killer running around."

I was quiet for a moment as I tried to come up with a casual lead-in to the questions I wanted to ask her. By now, Clover was napping. Looking like a complete angel, the little brat.

"So, Vicki..." I began. "I've been thinking about getting a Yorkie as a friend for Clover. Doesn't Denise Christensen have two?" Of course I knew they had Yorkies, but I wasn't sure how else to start the conversation.

Vicki laughed. "Well, yes, I guess you could say that. Though her father is usually the one stuck taking them to the vet. Denise just wants to be involved with the fun stuff like dressing them up for Halloween."

"Oh! Then do Sharon and Steve come in together?" I asked.

"No, it's usually just Steve, believe it or not. He's got a soft spot for those dogs. Calls them his 'babies.' It's really rather adorable."

My eyebrows shot straight up. I could not imagine a man

who communicates through grunts and grimaces having a thing for small dogs. Maybe he was a nicer guy than I gave him credit for.

"Huh! Well, you've certainly seen a side of him that I never have."

An idea started to form in my head. I gave Clover a thoughtful scritch, then asked, "Do Yorkies shed?"

Vicki's head tilted to the side. "Well, they're not generally known for shedding. This is primarily because they have a single layer of hair rather than a double coat of fur like many other breeds. Their hair is more like human hair in its texture. But if you have show dogs with long hair, you have to brush them every day. This can free any loose strands that have been caught up in the coat."

"Oh! I never knew some dogs had hair and not fur," I said.

Vicki started packing up her things. "Anyway, I'd recommend a second cat rather than a dog," she said. "I have to get to my next appointment, Maddie. Always great to see you and Clover!"

I gave her a hug, then picked up Clover's carrier. "I also have to get to a lunch date. Speaking of which, let's do lunch or coffee sometime. A year is too long to go without seeing each other," I said.

"Love to. You have my personal number. Call or text any time!"

AFTER THE VET, I DROPPED CLOVER AT HOME AND MET JEREMY at my favorite Greek restaurant to have lunch. It was a beautiful day, so we were sitting out on the patio which was decorated with crisp white and blue checked tablecloths and one of those large jugs of house red wine with a mesh sleeve.

"So, Jeremy... What can you tell me about the bloody

tennis bag that I brought in?" I know, I should have made some small talk first, but I just wasn't very good at that. Especially when I had a mystery on my mind! Thankfully, he was beginning to get to know me pretty well by now and wasn't fazed at all.

"Well, unfortunately, the bag was outside in the heat for hours before you rescued it from the tennis club dumpster. Heat is not good for DNA," he said. "I'm sure all of the rotten beef and other animal contaminants didn't help either. The blood was human, or parts of it were. But there's no way we'll be able to get any DNA or any other evidence from the bag."

I set down my Greek gyro in dismay. "What? I nearly got arrested for nothing?"

"I'm afraid so," he said, taking a bite of his garlic fries. "We can't even say for sure that it was Denise who threw the bag away, or why she really did it. Maybe she was trying to get rid of evidence, or maybe it was just as she said it was. A gross, dirty bag that she didn't want to keep." He looked at me for a moment, then added, "I wish you had talked to me before going to recover the bag."

I looked down at my hands. "I didn't want to waste your time. I could have been wrong about seeing blood on the bag."

"Or, I might have asked that you not go at all."

"Yeah. That, too," I said sheepishly. "Well, crap," I said. I proceeded to drown my sorrows in my delicious gyro. "I really messed things up." But at least I got lunch with Jeremy out of it!

"And before you ask, no, we don't have any results back from the racket yet. Shouldn't be long now, though," he said.

I nodded. "Good to know, thanks. I was wondering about that. And what about Brandon's stalking of Denise? Is there anything the police can do about it?"

"Unfortunately, no. He's stalking her in a very clever way. He's never somewhere just to be close to her. It's always something like picketing or attending a tennis match."

I sighed heavily. "Great. That's just great."

Jeremy started fiddling with his napkin and looked like there was something else that he wanted to say, but was he blushing? What could *that* be about?

I took a sip of my soda, trying to give him some time to get the words out. Finally, I gave up and said, "Something on your mind?" I gave him what I hoped was a reassuring smile.

"Ahem. Um, yes." He said, then turned as red as a beet! "Wanna go somewhere together? Like on a trip?"

For a moment, I was stunned. We haven't even kissed yet, and he wants to go away together? Then I realized that I was leaving him hanging.

"Oh, wow! Yes!" I said. "That sounds really great. Maybe after all of this, um, murder stuff is resolved? I don't want for you to have to take time away from work when so much is going on."

He smiled in relief. "Yes, that sounds reasonable. Good thinking. I guess start putting some thought into where you'd like to go. We can even bring Clover along, if you'd like?"

I grinned like the cat-loving girl that I am. Boy, this guy really knows the way to my heart.

I'm in trouble.

When the weather was nice, which was most of the year in Sycamore Cove, I liked to take Clover for an afternoon (or evening) walk to the beach. Clover was a special cat.

Today had become a very hot day, so I'd put off Clover's and my afternoon walk until things cooled down a bit. As soon as it did, I grabbed Clover's harness, her "hot sidewalk" booties, and her clear backpack carrier that had large breathing holes and a cooling fan inside.

Clover and I left by the side door next to the garage and followed the beautiful walking path that led toward the beach.

Clover walked ahead of me wearing her harness and little booties, sniffing and prancing in pure enjoyment of her surroundings. When she got tired, I put her in her backpack which allowed her to cool off, but still see everything around her. I felt the backpack shift as she tried to catch seagulls and butterflies.

By the time we got back, it was dusk. I started to take Clover out of her carrier, and was juggling the cat and my keys when I felt - or rather sensed - someone come up behind me.

Before I could react, they had grabbed me around the waist, lifting me into the air. I screamed and tried not to drop Clover.

I heard a man's voice growl into my ear, "Stop investigating this case! Just leave us alone!"

As I struggled with the cat and the man, Clover lashed out at my attacker with her claws.

Clover gave a high-pitch scream that ended in a long hiss. "*Mwerrrow-hisssss!!*"

She must have made contact, because he dropped me and yelled "Ow! Damn cat!"

I turned in time to see his hand move to his neck. He was masked, but I could tell it was the same man who I had encountered in the locker room. I was about to yell for help or perhaps grab his mask, when Mrs. Chan appeared behind him. The next thing I knew, she was thwacking him over the head with her cane!

"Augh!" he yelled, putting his hands over his head in an

attempt to protect himself from the barrage. Before we could do anything else, he ran off.

"Are you okay, dear?" Mrs. Chan asked. She barely seemed winded!

By now I had set Clover back in her carrier so she wouldn't run off in fright.

"Oh, my god, Mrs. Chan! That was amazing!" I said, still a little out of breath. I started dialing 911. I told them the situation, and they said they were on the way.

"Mrs. Chan, I should get Clover back inside the house while I wait for the police."

"You do that, dear," she said with a gentle pat on my arm. It was hard to believe that those thin, bony hands had just been beating the tar out of my attacker. "If they need to speak with me, they can find me in my house." With that, she slowly trundled off down the walk toward her home.

"Okay, bye!" I waved, still a bit in shock. "Thanks again!"

When the police came, I asked if they wanted to swab Clover's claws for evidence from the nasty scratch she gave the guy. I had been keeping Clover from licking off what seemed like blood and skin. They took samples, then told me they'd be in touch.

After they left, I cleaned Clover's claws, then gave her one of her favorite treats as a reward for her bravery. I then poured myself a glass of wine in reward for my own.

AFTER CALMING DOWN A BIT, I ASKED LIZZY TO COME OVER TO provide me with some comfort. She came over so quickly, I barely had time to open a second bottle of wine. Hey, the first bottle was nearly empty when I poured my glass!

"I can't believe you got attacked again!" Lizzy said, taking the glass of wine I handed to her.

We took a seat on the couch. Clover must have sensed my continued distress, because she immediately climbed onto my lap and curled up into a ball. There's also the possibility that she needed some comfort as much as I did. The attack had to have freaked her out as well, so I stroked her fur, slowly and calmly. I was rewarded with a throaty purr.

"Well, I don't know that I'd call the original incident in the locker rooms an 'attack' exactly, though it felt like one. He just knocked me over because I was in his way. I was definitely in the wrong place at the wrong time," I said.

"Hmm. Semantics aside, who do you think it was?" she asked.

"It had to be the same guy from the locker room. He had on a similar-looking, full-face mask, and seemed to be of the same build. It just had to be the same guy."

"Who are the males on our suspect list?" she asked.

"Other than the mystery man himself, just Coach Masayuki and Brandon," I said. "And I think Coach Masayuki is the wrong body type. But Brandon could definitely be our mystery man."

I took another sip of wine. "You know, now that I have a little bit of wine in me, I just remembered something."

"Oh? What?" Lizzy asked.

"When he grabbed me, he said 'leave *us* alone,' not 'leave *me* alone.'"

"Are you sure?" Lizzy asked. "Could he have said 'leave *this* alone'? Because using 'us' seems a little weird. I mean, who is 'us'?"

"Hmm. Maybe you're right. In the heat of the moment, I most certainly could have misunderstood what he said. 'This' does make a lot more sense," I agreed, taking another fortifying sip of Cabernet.

"Well, I'm just glad you're okay! Crazy that it was Mrs.

Chan who came to your rescue. I mean, who knew she had it in her?"

We both laughed at this. It felt really good to laugh.

Clover opened one eye and said, "Meow."

"Oh! And you certainly helped, too, Clover!" Lizzy amended.

I swear, sometimes I feel like Clover understands us.

"Can I just make one request?" Lizzy asked.

"Sure."

"Please, please, *please* get yourself a security camera system installed?"

"Yes. I will most definitely do that," I said.

Chapter Thirteen

Tuesday, October 14

The following day, my grandfather came over to install my new security camera system. It had cost a pretty penny, but it would be worth it. At least the labor was free!

When he rang the doorbell, I ran downstairs to get it.

"Pops! You're here!"

"Hey there, Sunshine!" He gave me a huge smile and even bigger bear hug.

Clover had also run downstairs to greet him.

"And there's my little Four Leaf Clover!" He bent down to pick her up and pulled her into his arms for a good ruffling. I could hear her purring from where I stood.

"That's my little, furry, great grandchild," he laughed and gently set her down.

The three of us went upstairs.

"Can I get you some coffee, Pops?" I asked, pouring a fresh cup for myself from the pot.

"Ooh! Yes, please. I haven't had mine yet," he said, setting his tool kit on the coffee table.

I handed him a fresh cup with lots of sugar and cream, just the way he liked it.

We chatted for a bit, catching up on life. I told him all that was going on with the investigation, and Jeremy.

"Sounds like your relationship with Jeremy might be getting serious," he said with a wink.

I blushed. "Yeah, well, we'll see." I cleared my throat. "So, let me grab the camera equipment so you can get started."

A few hours later, I had a camera in my garage, one pointed at my ground floor patio (and doorbell), as well as cameras on the kitchen and bedroom floors pointing toward the second and third story balconies. He also installed sensors on all of the windows.

Grandpas are just the best.

~

THAT AFTERNOON, AFTER A NAP WITH CLOVER, I DECIDED TO stalk Brandon. I'd have to find him first, but I wanted to follow him around for a while. See what he did with his time.

Hey... if he could stalk Denise, I could stalk him! Right?

Right.

I knew Brandon was in the habit of getting donuts every day for his "picketing parties," so I decided the best place to start would be at Maison du Croissant. Based on what Juste had said, I knew he would be arriving in the afternoon, so I planned to have coffee and a chocolate croissant while I waited in my car.

The only snag would be when I eventually needed a restroom.

But for now, I was content. I had borrowed Lizzy's car since it didn't stand out like mine.

I kept my eye on the front of the croissant shop while I

sipped my coffee. Lately, I had been craving chocolate, so my chocolate croissant was paired with a cafe mocha, complete with a large dollop of whipped cream and a chocolate syrup drizzle. Yum.

I was starting to nod off into a carb coma when I spotted Brandon's VW Bug parking in front of the bakery. He hopped out of his car and went into the store. A few minutes later, he came out with a box of what I assumed to be donuts in his hand, and a croissant clamped between his teeth. I guess between the donuts and his car keys, he had run out of hands. I waited until he was in the car before I started mine up.

The first place he went was to the tennis courts on Temple. Made sense, I supposed. To my surprise, he didn't spend very long there. I didn't even have to get out of the car to see that he took his picket signs and donuts to one of the courts and set up on a bench. After only about thirty minutes, he closed the donut box, grabbed his picket signs, and went back to his car.

His next stop was another set of tennis courts a few miles east of the Temple courts.

I parked in the shade of some trees and watched Brandon get out of his car. Before grabbing the donut box and his picketing signs, he walked toward a blue BMW. It was Denise's car! The top was down, and I saw him look inside. He looked around, then ran his finger down the side of the car. Yuck.

Quickly, he headed back to his car and took the donuts and signs onto the courts.

I got out of the car and sneaked my way along the fence to see what was going on. Brandon had set up his picketing at a bench near the court Denise was on.

It seemed Denise noticed him (how could she not, once

he started yelling about "courts for everyone"), but she did an impressive job of ignoring him.

With a sigh, I went back to my car to wait.

I felt badly for Denise, and I also wished I could get out there to play with her! It was a beautiful day.

About an hour later, Denise left the courts and Brandon left shortly thereafter.

Where to now, I wondered.

Turns out, it was The Alibi. The same bar where Rick had "interrogated" Brandon about Coach Matteo. At least he didn't follow Denise home!

But it meant that this was going to be a long wait.

I gave Lizzy a quick call to let her know I still out and about and had ended up at The Alibi. I asked her to feed and water her "niece." Aka, Clover.

I figured this would be a good time for a bathroom break. I hopped online and ordered some food and drink for pick-up. When it was ready I went into the bar, went to the restroom, then picked up my meal. Thankfully, Brandon was sitting at the bar and didn't seem to notice me. Not that he'd necessarily realize that I was following him!

I headed back out to my car and ate my food. It really bothered me that Brandon could just follow Denise whenever she was playing tennis. Something needed to be done about this!

A few hours later, I had dozed off. Thankfully, Brandon's VW Bug was quite loud when it started up, so I was able to wake up in time to follow him home.

Unfortunately, he drove very carefully Gand at a reasonable speed, so I couldn't report him for potential drunk driving.

Eventually, we ended up at a small, one-story tract home in a neighborhood of larger models. It looked rather lonely at the end of the cul-de-sac. I stayed back as soon as I realized he was almost home. Too bad it was a dead end. I couldn't just drive past nonchalantly.

When he finally went inside, I wearily drove home.

Once there, I picked up Clover and took her upstairs to bed with me.

Chapter Fourteen

Tuesday, October 14

The next day, I decided that I needed to have a chat with Brandon. He sorta fit the build of my attacker, and he definitely didn't like me. But what really bothered me was his stalking of Denise and his behavior at the funeral. It had been very odd, to say the least.

Now that I knew where he lived, I drove to his house. This time I took my own car, since I wasn't trying to blend in anymore. I couldn't figure out what he did for a living. He always seemed to be at the tennis courts, the bakery, or the bar. So I decided to come later in the evening, to see if I could catch him.

Luckily, I could see Brandon's VW Bug parked on the street in front of his house, so at least I didn't make the drive for nothing. I parked on the street behind his car and walked up the steep driveway.

The entryway to his front door was an overgrown patio area which was enclosed by a wooden fence with a matching, latched-entry gate. Only his gate wasn't latched or even closed. It sat ajar.

Well, that was odd. The gate had a sign on it that said, "No

Solicitors," but that didn't apply to me, right? I didn't see any sort of intercom or a camera door bell, so I walked through the gate into the small garden-like patio filled with ferns, short palms, and a two-seater table near the front door. The windows had white shutters which were closed. But I didn't need to see inside the house to know if Brandon was home.

He was. Kinda.

I spotted him as soon as I was halfway to the front door. That door was also open, and he was laying on the ground, face-down, halfway in and halfway out of the house. His head and torso were outside of the house, and a pool of blood had formed around his belly.

Gingerly, taking great care not to disturb anything, I reached down to feel his neck for a pulse. Nope. No pulse. And his body was cold.

My heart sank as I realized I'd just found another body. I was going to get a complex!

I stood back up. From this angle, and due to his being face down on the ground, I couldn't tell how he'd died, but it certainly didn't appear to be a natural death.

Unfortunately, this meant that I had to call my sister. Thankfully, as her sister, I had her direct line.

"Chief Murphy," she answered immediately.

"Hey Sis," I said. I could almost hear her groan. I never called her at work.

"What's wrong?" she asked, her voice dripped with suspicion.

"Why does something have to be wrong?" I asked, in an attempt to delay the inevitable.

"Maddie?" she prodded.

"Okay, yes. Something is wrong. I found another body. It's that pickleball guy, Brandon."

"Are you in danger?" she asked. "If you think the killer might still be there, I want you to leave immediately."

I have to admit, I was pleased that her worry for me outweighed her frustration with my tendency to get into these types of situations.

"I'm not in danger," I said. "From the looks of things, his body has been there quite a while. The pool of blood was dry and when I tried to take his pulse, he was cold to the touch."

I heard her sigh heavily over the phone line.

"Okay then, I want you to go sit in your car until we get there. Do not touch anything."

I rolled my eyes. Like I didn't know that. Without so much as a goodbye, she hung up the phone.

While I waited, I had a quick look around without moving my feet. As per Annabelle's directive, I didn't touch anything. Nothing seemed out of place. I got excited when I noticed a camera door bell, but then saw some sort of film on the camera lens. Maybe done by the killer.

I worked my way back toward the driveway, careful to retrace my steps as well as I could remember, then sat in my car waiting for Annabelle and her forensics team.

Ooh! That meant I'd get to see Jeremy! Though not under the best circumstances. We'd have to stop meeting like this. Maybe go out for ice cream or something.

I was starting to get bored when three cars pulled up. Two marked police vehicles, and an unmarked car with two forensic techs in it. One was Jeremy. I got out to greet him.

He exited the unmarked car and came up to me with a smirk on his face. "So, you did it again, huh? Found a body? You're a magnet for trouble!"

"Hey! I just wanted to talk to him," I said. "Sounds like I was on the right track, too, if someone wanted him dead. Too bad I didn't get to talk to him first."

"Oh, no no. I don't want to chance you getting on the radar of another killer!" Jeremy said.

"We don't know that there's another killer. Could be the same guy that killed Coach Matteo," I said.

"Well, I need to look at the crime scene before I can voice an opinion on that," he said.

We turned to see the rest of the team making their way up the driveway. Annabelle gestured to Jeremy to get a move on. He said a quick goodbye, then jogged in their direction.

Annabelle walked over to me.

"Did you touch anything? See anyone?" she asked.

"No," I said. "But I did see some kind of plastic film on the doorbell camera. I looked around for a weapon-" Annabelle glared at me. I held up my hands defensively. "Just looked! Didn't move and didn't touch! But I also didn't see anything that might be a weapon," I said with disappointment.

She nodded. "Okay, Maddie. Go home. We'll talk later."

What? I wanted to stick around! "But I-"

She pointed at my car and gave me the big sister glare. "Home. Now." She started to walk away, but turned back and gave me a quick hug. "I'm glad you're okay," she said, then turned toward the house and trudged up the driveway.

I huffed in frustration, but obeyed her demand and went to my car. Well, that was a bust. Except that it sure did change my suspect board!

I had to call Lizzy and Rick!

And I'd have to find time to come back to Brandon's. Maybe in a few days... after the dust had settled a bit.

LIZZY AND RICK CAME OVER IN A HEARTBEAT WHEN I TOLD them I'd found Brandon's body.

Now we were all sitting in my living room, grabbing the snacks I'd laid out on the coffee table.

"Wow, Sis, you really do have a knack for finding dead bodies!" Rick said.

I sighed. It wasn't a pleasant thought, but I couldn't really argue with it either.

"Hey! She's already had a rough day," Lizzy said. "You don't need to make her feel worse."

Rick frowned. "Oh, sorry. You're right."

"But you're not wrong," I said. "It has been a weird day. And they wouldn't even let me stick around to find out what happened to him!"

"Well, I guess we can take him off our suspects board," Rick said.

Like last time, I had set up the board on the stand on the other side of the coffee table. Clover had already given the suspect board a thorough inspection. She also enjoyed her own small samples of the snacks I'd set out. Her approval came in the form of a leg rub, after which she had gone to sit in her favorite chair to listen in on our discussion.

I stood up and walked over to the board.

"Actually," I said. "What we really need is to give him his own board. Now that he's been murdered, or so I assume, we'll need a separate investigation. We can't assume the two murders are connected. That introduces bias. But, if during our investigation we find that there is overlap, that itself will be telling."

Lizzy nodded. "Ah, yes. I see your point. But what if he's the one who killed Matteo? How could they ever prove it if he's dead? It's not like he can confess."

"Well, we are still waiting on the DNA evidence from the racket, and results from the other evidence they found at the scene like the blood spatter and footprints. Maybe they'll find something that will link him to that crime," I said, sitting down again. "But what I really want to do is get back to Brandon's house and have a look around for clues."

"Isn't that what our sister is doing right now?" Rick asked.

"I know," I said. "And I'm sure she'll do a great job. But you also know that in addition to my uncanny knack for finding bodies, I have a tendency to find evidence that others overlook."

Both Lizzy and Rick nodded in agreement at this.

That settled, I made a copy of Brandon's photo and added it to a second board that I'd set up next to Matteo's. Now he was on both boards: once as the victim, and once as a potential suspect.

"So," I said. "Who are our suspects?"

"We're gonna need a bigger board," Rick said.

We all laughed. Then sobered up when we realized how much work we had ahead of us.

Rick said, "Maybe he made some enemies when picketing?"

"Or perhaps he was making moves on someone's girlfriend?" Lizzy suggested.

"Hey! What about road rage?" Rick asked.

Lizzy looked at him sideways. "And they followed him home to kill him?"

"What? It could happen," Rick said.

We all nodded in agreement.

"True, true," I said.

"What about Steve?" Lizzy suggested. "It seemed there was something serious going on between them at Matteo's funeral."

My eyebrows went up. "Right! It did seem like there was some bad blood there. Good idea." I got up and placed Steve's name on Brandon's board. I scratched my chin. "We just don't know *why*."

Rick raised his hand. "I vote for Denise."

Lizzy and I looked at him in shock.

"What?" he asked. "You yourselves said a woman can do

some serious damage. Maybe Denise got tired of being stalked. Took matters into her own hands."

"I have to admit, that's a pretty good possibility," Lizzy said. "It would have been easy for her to get Brandon to open the door to her. Then BANG! She shoots him and runs away."

"I think someone would have heard a gun shot," Rick said.

I sighed. I really hated the idea that she could feel so trapped that she'd have to do something that drastic. And life-changing. For both of them.

"All right," I said, standing at the board. "We have 'picketing,' 'jealousy,' 'road rage,' 'Steve,' and 'Denise.'" I turned back to Lizzy and Rick. "Everything is fair game right now. So how about we set the boards aside for the moment. Keep thinking about potential suspects for both murders. Let things percolate."

I got nods of relieved agreement.

"Great! So who wants to go over to Brandon's house with me when they release the crime scene?" I asked with a big smile.

Chapter Fifteen

Thursday, October 16

I stood at the back of what was technically a press conference. However, due to the fact that this was a small town and they were about to announce a second murder, it felt like the whole town was in attendance.

Once again, my sister stood at the front of the room with her team, waiting for the room to quiet. On days like this, I held no envy in my heart for the success she has had in her chosen career.

The room quieted, and she looked out at the crowd.

"Good afternoon. My name is Annabelle Quinn Murphy, Chief of Police. I'm sorry to have to announce that we have found another body."

At this, the room rumbled with gasps and low-voiced conversations.

"We will not be releasing any specific details at this time, as this is an ongoing murder investigation."

More rumblings throughout the room.

"We can only tell you that the victim was a male, and a resident of our community. It appears that he died sometime yesterday afternoon. I can't promise to have all the answers right now, but I can take questions."

The hands of every reporter in the room shot up. My sister tried not to roll her eyes.

"Yes, Matt?" she asked, pointing at a reporter sitting toward the front row.

"Thank you, Chief. Do we have a serial killer on our hands?" Matt asked.

"No, we do not," Annabelle replied. "And I'd appreciate it if you'd take care not to spread stories to that effect. However, these are both still active investigations, so I'm limited as to how many details I can share at this time."

At this, the room got pretty loud. What's worse? A single serial killer or two killers in a small town?

Annabelle gave everyone a few minutes to digest this, then called for silence. Hands shot up again.

"Yes, Rita?"

"Do we think there's a connection between these murders?" Rita asked.

"Yes, we have reason to believe the cases are connected, but that's all I can say right now. We have a suspect in custody and will have more information for you after we've spoken to this individual. Thank you for your time. That's all for now." She took her notes and left the podium, followed by her officers.

At that, we were dismissed.

Then it hit me.

Wait, what? They had a suspect in custody? Who? Why hadn't I heard about this before the press conference from either Annabelle or Jeremy?

Dying of curiosity, I was looking around for Jeremy when from the other side of the room, I was spotted by Steve and Sharon. Sharon caught my eye and waved, pushing her way through the crowd toward me, closely followed by her husband. I sighed to myself and waited for her to come to me.

"Mads! Can you believe this?" she asked, breathless with excitement. Steve stood a good distance behind her with his usual grumpy expression.

"No, I can't believe someone else is dead!" I said, trying to be polite. "I wish they'd tell us who it is." I wasn't about to tell her that I'd also found this body!

"It has to be a serial killer, don't you think? I mean, what are the odds there are *two* killers in our little town? And Steve and I went out for dinner last night! We were out and about when the killer was striking! We could have been killed!"

"I'm going to wait in the car," Steve said. "Don't take too long, Sharon." He turned on his heel and walked away.

I had no idea what to say in response to her serial killer theory, so I was relieved to see Jeremy making his way toward me. I looked over her shoulder and called to him.

"Jeremy! Thanks for finding me. Excuse me, Sharon. I have to talk to Jeremy."

Sharon stuck her hand out and he took it, like the polite guy he was. "I don't believe we've met," she said. "So rare to see a new face in a small town. For all we know, you could be the serial killer!" She laughed and gave him a big smile. "Just kidding, of course. My name is Sharon Christensen. I own the knitting shop in town."

"Nice to meet you. Please excuse us," he said, deftly guiding me away with a hand at the small of my back.

"Bye Sharon! Talk later!" I said, with a wave. She gave a small frown as we walked away. No doubt she wanted to grill him for information on the new murder.

To be fair, I wanted to do the same thing.

We stopped in the crowded hallway outside the press room. The room was not designed to hold that many people, so the overflow went into the hall and the lobby. Officers were now trying to clear the crowd as quickly as possible.

Jeremy held me by my shoulders in an attempt to keep me steady as we got jostled by the crowd.

"Why don't you go to the break room and get yourself a coffee and a donut," he said. "I'll see what I can find out." The way he looked at me, I could tell something was wrong.

"Everything okay, Jeremy?" I asked, concerned.

"It could be better," he said. "We'll catch up later, okay?"

My eyes narrowed a bit, but I just said, "Okay." Then impulsively give him a quick kiss on the cheek. His hand went to his cheek in surprise.

I walked down the hall toward the break room - which unfortunately happened to be the same hallway that led to the room where I was interrogated a few days ago. I shivered in recollection.

At that moment, I stopped in shock as I saw an officer leading Coach Masayuki in cuffs into that same room!

Before I could stop myself, I called out to him. "Coach!"

He had been looking down at the floor. When he heard me call out, he looked up at me with wide eyes.

"Madeline! Tell them I'm innocent! I'm not a killer!"

I STOOD THERE, STUNNED, AS I WATCHED THEM LEAD HIM INTO the interrogation room. His pleading eyes followed me for as long as possible before they closed the door behind them.

I looked longingly at the door to the little room behind the two-way mirror. But I knew that not only would I not be able to get in there, but that I'd better scoot before anyone else spotted me in the hallway.

Quickly, I power-walked my way to the break room. Technically, it was only for employees, but I'd been here often enough with my sister that I didn't feel like too much of an intruder.

I made myself a frothy cappuccino and grabbed a Bavarian cream donut. God, I loved this break room! I found a quiet table in the corner and sat down to wait with my caffeine and sugar.

Who would want to kill Brandon?

Although Masayuki had been a suspect of mine early on, I had come to believe in my heart that he couldn't have done it. And while he may not be perfect, Coach Matteo's broken rib was proof of that, killing someone was just not something he would do.

I know Brandon was a pain in the patootie, but what could he have done to get himself killed? Surely not just the picketing of tennis courts? Maybe it had something to do with him stalking Denise?

I was still mulling this over when Jeremy walked in about an hour later. By now, I was practically buzzing with too much sugar, caffeine, and eagerness to know the inside scoop. I looked up at him in anticipation.

"Hi!" I said quietly, even though we were the only people in the break room.

"Hey! Thanks for waiting. Sorry that took so long," he said. He took a closer look at me. "Hmm. I think maybe you've had enough coffee and sugar for a while." He laughed softly.

"Yeah, guilty as charged," I said with an eye twitch. Mmm. Sexy.

Jeremy looked around the empty room, then said, "They've arrested Masayuki Noguchi for the murder of Brandon Lewis. They just finished interrogating him and it's not looking good." He shook his head in dismay.

I nodded. "I know. I saw them take him in cuffs! He called

out to me that he didn't kill anyone. I was in shock! Still am..."
I said.

"Unfortunately, Brandon was stabbed. They found one of
Masayuki's special sushi knives at the scene."

"What?!" I said, a little too loudly. "Sorry!" I whispered. "First
of all, he wouldn't kill anyone," I said in a normal voice. "Even
someone as annoying as Brandon. And secondly, he wouldn't be
stupid enough to use one of his super-unique knives and then go
and leave it at the scene of the crime! No way. Ridiculous." I was
shaking my head emphatically. "And how did I miss a knife?"

"Well, it was dumped in the thick hedges that surround
the front of the house. It would have been hard to find unless
you were actively looking for it. Which we were."

"Doesn't he have an alibi?" I asked.

"No," Jeremy said. "He claims he was asleep and alone at
his house. His fingerprints were the only ones on the knife."

"Oh, no. This is terrible. Poor Coach Masayuki!" I felt
myself tearing up in sympathy.

"They had to arrest him, but there will be a full investigation. If he's innocent, we'll figure that out."

"He *is* innocent. I just know it." At the moment, I was
quite disappointed in the justice system. "But I can see why
Annabelle believes the cases are connected. And it sure seems
likely that they're the work of two different killers. Although
the crimes were quite different and the M.O.s were, too, we
have three male racket players: two are now dead and one
has been arrested."

"Agreed," Jeremy said. "And while both were personal acts
of violence, it seems to be that's where the similarities end.
Oh, I almost forgot! The lab did get some DNA off of
Clover's claws from your attack the other day. We've sent it
out for analysis. Hopefully we'll be able to match it with
someone."

"That's some good news, at least," I said.

We sat quietly for a while, lost in our thoughts. Then Jeremy said, "Well, I'd better get back to work. You should head home. Get some rest. You've had a trying afternoon."

"Yeah. I feel exhausted," I said. "Despite the coffee and donuts."

We said our goodbyes, and I headed out to my car. As I did, I gave Lizzy a call.

"Lizzy! They've just arrested Coach Masayuki for Brandon's murder! We have to get over to Brandon's house. There has to be something there they've missed."

Chapter Sixteen

Friday, October 17

The next day, Lizzy and I took her car to Brandon's. No sense in advertising who's breaking into Brandon's yard by parking my car out front. Besides, is it really trespassing if the owner of the house is dead?

With that justification in my mind, I said, "I'm sure they did a fine job inside the house, but I wonder if they thought to look around the back? There isn't even a gate or anything blocking access to the side or back yards!"

Lizzy followed me as we quickly made our way to the back yard via the side of the house. The side yard was empty, so we headed straight to the overgrown back yard.

Much like the front patio, the back was overgrown with trees, bushes, some weeds, and a long wax privet hedge that acted like a wall between the house's yard and whatever might be on the other side. The hedge was so high, it was hard to see anything. The smell of the flowers was sugary-sweet on a warm day like this one.

Hidden behind heavy foliage, I spotted what looked like a small garage with room for only one car. It had one of those old, wood-flap-style garage doors, rather than one of the more modern segmented aluminum doors with the electric opener.

"Wonder what's in there? Hey? Does that lock look broken to you?" I asked, pointing to a cheap lock that was looped through a thin metal bar. I waggled my eyebrows at her.

"Yep. Sure does," Lizzy lied.

There are many reasons Lizzy and I have been best friends since we were five years old. One of those reasons is that she always has my back.

I looked around for a tool to pry open the lock. When a crowbar or screwdriver didn't magically appear, I opted for a large rock. That did the trick.

We both held our breath as we lifted the garage door.

Despite being a very old garage door, someone had recently oiled the hinges because it opened with barely a whisper.

There was something large under an old army-camo tarp. Something car-sized.

"Help me lift this tarp!" I grabbed one side and she grabbed the other. Under the tarp, we saw the back side of a very nice car. I peeked in the back window and saw a few suitcases.

"Hmm," Lizzy said. "Wonder where he got this nice car?"

"And I wonder where he was going in it?" I asked. "It looks packed for a trip."

I took a few photos then we covered it back up and closed the garage. I tossed the broken lock into the deep belly of the wax privet. We headed back toward the front of the house.

"Come on. Let's get a quick look in the trash!" I said. "The bins are on the street, so they're fair game."

"Eww! Why?" Lizzy asked as we walked toward the bins.

"In all the Hallmark mysteries, there always seems to be

something interesting to be found in people's trash," I said, handing her some nitrile gloves I had taken with me.

"Like what?" Lizzy asked, pulling on her gloves.

"Their secrets!" I said, lifting the top off the recycle bin. "Important papers and receipts, weapons, discarded crime scene clothes..."

"Rabid raccoons..." Lizzy said.

Inside the recycle bin, we saw a few plastic garbage bags which appeared to be filled with papers. I tore one open and could see a bunch of official-looking paperwork. Score!

"Quick, Lizzy! Grab a few of these and put them in the car," I said, grabbing one bag in each hand. She grabbed two bags, stuck them in the car, then came back for two more.

We headed to my house with our paper treasure.

LIZZY AND I TOOK OUR LOOT - OKAY, TRASH - FROM Brandon's house back to my place. We divvied up the bags and spread the papers out around my living room. Thankfully, the papers were not dirty or smelly.

While we sifted through papers of all kinds - electric bills, medical bills, bank statements, credit card statements - Clover was having a blast jumping on the pile of papers like it was a pile of leaves instead. It was adorable! If a bit disruptive. Then, she got a little overworked and started tearing at some of the papers with her claws and teeth like a tiny, furry shredder.

"Hey, hey, hey there little girlie! That's potential evidence in a murder case you're shredding there!" I said, grabbing the papers back gingerly. I've been known to get my fingers shredded when trying to confiscate items from the jaws and claws of my little Lucky Clover.

As I tried to flatten out the papers, my eye was drawn to

the bank statement I held in my hands. There was a definite pattern there. Once a week, for the last three weeks, there was a deposit of five thousand dollars into Brandon's checking account.

"Bingo! Lizzy! Try to find more bank statements that look like this." I showed her the paper and pointed out the bank's logo, name, and account number. "Good job, Clover!" I said, giving her a pat on the head.

"Meow!" Clover said.

"Who gets statements mailed anymore?" Lizzy asked, as she ripped open another bag.

"I don't know," I said. "Although, I remember one bank that no matter what I did, they kept mailing me paper statements. I had to invest in a shredder."

We rifled through the papers looking for more of the same. I put our findings in order of oldest to most recent date.

"Ha! Yes!" I said in triumph. "Look. Before Matteo died, Brandon was always broke. Lots of overdrafts. Barely making it from paycheck to paycheck. Then BAM. He's getting thousands of dollars from someone. And it appears that these types of deposits were being made to *multiple* accounts!" I quickly did some math. "I'm seeing at least fifty grand in payments here."

"Oh, wow. That's a lot of money! What does it mean? He was blackmailing someone?" Lizzy asked.

"Yes," I said. "And it means that Brandon didn't commit the murder of Matteo. It means he *witnessed* it."

～

"Brandon was blackmailing someone!" I said, excited at the information I had to share.

My sister and I sat in her office, and she looked at me skeptically at this news.

"Blackmail," she said. I could hear the doubt in her voice.

I nodded.

"And you know this... how, exactly?" she asked.

Hmm. Right. That.

"Okay, well, don't get mad." Her eyes narrowed at me. "But I might have gone back to Brandon's house after you cleared the crime scene." The last sentence came out in a rush before I could lose my nerve. I waited for the lecture. The yelling.

Nothing.

Maybe she was getting numb to my antics? I couldn't stand the silence anymore.

"It's no one's property now, right? I can't be trespassing if the owner is dead."

She blinked at me slowly. "It *is* trespassing, actually. Tell me about the blackmail. What did you find?"

I launched into an explanation about the nice car in Brandon's garage filled with luggage, and the trash with the bank statements.

She thought about this for a few minutes, then, "I'm in no way condoning what you did. It was dangerous and potentially illegal in ten different ways. But..." She sighed heavily. "Good work."

I beamed with pride. "Thanks, Annabelle. Can you use this information? Maybe whomever it was he was blackmailing was his killer! Can you find out?"

"It will take some time, but yes. I can find out who was on the other end of those transactions. I know my team looked through the trash for weapons and clothing, but I'll have to have a conversation with them as to why they didn't collect the bank statements, or find the car hidden in the back yard garage." Her lips pinched together in displeasure.

Uh, oh. I hope I didn't just get Jeremy into trouble.

Chapter Seventeen

Saturday, October 18

I was working at the shop with my assistant manager, Nikki, when Sharon walked in with Steve. He hung near the front door while Sharon made her way around the store fingering rackets, bags, and gloves, looking like she had something on her mind.

Clover was doing her best to ignore both of them.

Nikki started to offer her assistance, but I said, "I got this one." She nodded and went back behind the counter.

"Hi Sharon!" I said. As Steve wasn't paying any attention to me, I didn't feel the need to acknowledge him either.

"Mads, hi! I'm thinking of getting a racket like the one Denise got. I think I have racket envy," she said with a weak laugh.

"Okay, sure. Well, hers was a Head racket. You can find them over here," I said, leading her to a display near the register. I liked to keep the more expensive items deeper in the store and out of reach whenever possible. I grabbed the tool I used to take rackets off the wall hangers and selected a Head racket in a color I thought she would like. I handed it to her.

She looked at it dutifully, but I could see that her mind was on something else. For a minute, she stared at the racket with unfocused eyes, as though she was seeing something else entirely. I'd swear I saw her start to tear up. Then, clearing her throat, her focus sharpened again and she looked up at me.

"Your sister is the Chief of Police, right?" she asked.

"Yes," I said, caution in my voice. Just where was this going? "Why do you ask?"

"Well, you see, Matteo... That is, Coach Matteo, meant a lot to me." She looked nervously back at her husband, who was still near the front of the store. I noticed he kept scratching at his neck. "Anyway," she continued, "I was wondering if she's made any progress in the case. I mean, I know what the papers say, but I was hoping that you might have the inside scoop. Like, do they have any real suspects?"

Huh. I'd have to answer this carefully. As I did, in fact, have the inside scoop, I hadn't been paying all that much attention to what the papers had been saying.

"Well," I said, "for a while, they thought that pickleball guy had a hand in the coach's death, but they're obviously revisiting that now that he's been killed. They did question Coach Masayuki, but I'm sure you saw that in the news." Sharon nodded her head. "I can't say where they're at with that line of investigation though."

I heard a hiss from Clover and looked over to see that Steve had wandered close to her perch. He saw me looking and said, "Cats don't like me." He gave Clover a dirty look, then made his way back toward the front of the store again. I glared at Steve then turned back to Sharon.

Sharon fingered the strings of the racket nervously. "Yeah, that's all the stuff I knew already. Well, thanks anyway, I guess." She handed the racket back to me. "I think I'll wait on the racket. I'm still not sure which one I want the most." She gave me a small smile.

After an awkward silence, I asked, "Hey! Are you going to have a booth for your yarn shop at the Harvest Festival?"

This perked up her mood. "Oh, yes! I'm going to have some skeins for sale and I've asked my assistant to give hands-on lessons on how to knit cup cozies." A big smile lit up her face.

"Great idea! I'll be sure to stop by your booth," I said. "Thanks for coming in today. You know where to find me when you've made a decision on your racket."

She nodded, then headed out the front door, followed by Steve.

Chapter Eighteen

Sunday, October 19

It was time for Sycamore Cove's Fall Harvest Festival! My second favorite time of year (tennis tournaments being my first, naturally).

I came with my little posse of friends: Rick and Lizzy, of course, and Denise - the newest addition. The night was warmed by the gentle Santa Ana winds that we get in our area this time of year.

"Hey, you guys," Lizzy said. "I need to go check in at my candle booth before I join up with you for tonight's festivities. Gotta make sure my assistant manager has everything she needs to cover things for me."

"Sounds good, Lizzy! I think we're gonna go check out the food booths. I'm famished!" I said.

"You're always famished, Sis," Rick said with a laugh.

"Can't argue with that," Denise said with a shy smile. She was new to our group, so she was still nervous about what was cool to say and what wasn't. Rick laughed heartily at her joke, and her smile got wider and more genuine.

"Okay, okay. But don't tell me you're not hungry, too. Just smell all of that amazing food!" I said, leading them toward a line of ten or so food vendors. We had representation from some of our favorite restaurants and food trucks. I opted for the hot-dog-on-a-stick booth, getting two corn dogs and a freshly squeezed lemonade. Rick went for the Korean barbecue, and Denise went the healthier route with a Greek salad.

We took our food and sat down at one of the many picnic tables they had set up between the food vendor booths. I finished my corn dogs before the others were done eating, so I just sat there taking in the wonderful fall decor of pumpkins, scarecrows, and black cats (my favorite).

It wasn't too long before we were joined by Lizzy who had gone straight for dessert. She was carrying an "elephant ear," which was really just a large, flat buttermilk biscuit. She got hers with cinnamon sugar and honey.

"I figure, why waste calories on dinner when I can just indulge in dessert!" she said, sitting down next to me.

"Life is short," Rick said. "Eat dessert first."

"Exactly," she replied, smiling at him.

"Well, you can afford the calories. Your metabolism is to die for," I said.

Denise looked down at her food. I guess mentioning death wasn't the best topic of conversation. I quickly changed the subject.

"Hey, Denise! What's your favorite thing to do at the festival?" I asked.

She looked up again with a smile. "Oh, I love looking at all of the luxury goods like hand-made soaps, perfumes, and candles." She looked over at Lizzy. "Your booth has always been one of my favorites."

"Oh, wow! Thanks, Denise! That's really great to hear," Lizzy said, grinning from ear to ear. "I put a lot of work into that booth. Making candles in advance, filling custom orders from the festival... it's all very time-consuming, but well worth it. I really get to know people from the community. I even get repeat customers from year to year."

We finished our meals and threw out our trash.

"Let's walk around a bit," I said. "Check out the booths, decorations, pumpkins, and the bonfire!" I said. I pulled my coat on as it was getting colder now that the sun had fully set. It was a waning crescent moon tonight. Perfect for a festival such as this.

"Where's Jeremy tonight?" Denise asked me.

"Oh! He gets off work soon. He's gonna meet us here." I looked at my phone for a text for probably the tenth time since we arrived. Nothing yet. Sigh.

Since we were already in the food area, we went to the Maison du Croissant first.

"Mads! Good to see you. Can I interest you in a Rustic Peach Galette?" He held up a beautiful peach tart-looking thing. My mouth immediately started to water even though I had just eaten two corn dogs. He gave us each a sample of the pastry, and we *oohed* and *aahed* in appreciation.

"I'll take one of those!" Rick said.

"I'd like to get something a little less sweet," Denise said.

"I have some Cranberry Brie Pinwheels," Juste said. At her nod of enthusiasm, he bagged one for her.

"I think I want something with pumpkin," I said.

He looked around his booth and came up with a little, square pumpkin dump cake. "*Voila!*" he said, handing it to me with a flourish.

"Merci!" I said, taking my treat. "Thank you! Best of luck to you tonight."

We took our yummy snacks and went to find Marcy's book booth. It was more toward the edge of the fair grounds, but we found her easily enough. She had a large, open box decorated like a book that said, "Donate your books here!"

"Hello Marcy!" I said, pulling two small donation books

out of my purse. When I dropped them into the box, it sounded a bit hollow. I peeked over the edge and was dismayed to see that there were only a few books at the bottom of the box. "Oh, no!" I said with a sad pout. "Well, it's still early yet, right?"

"Yeah, I guess so," Marcy said. "You live and you learn! I meant to put up a sign about the donation box at the shop, but kept forgetting. That might have helped."

Lizzy reached out to give Marcy a pat on the shoulder. "Maybe just make it a year-round service at the shop," she said. Marcy nodded in agreement.

Next up was Kay's Koffee for a hot beverage to go with our quickly disappearing pastries. Not surprisingly, there was a long line, so we queued up and chatted aimlessly as we slowly got closer to the front.

Finally, I was able to order one of my favorite beverages. A cafe mocha with an extra shot of espresso! And whipped cream, of course. "How's business, Kay?"

Kay looked frazzled, but also happy. "Great! I've had some fantastic feedback on my holiday specials."

"Speaking of," Lizzy said. "Can I get a peppermint latte please?"

Rick got a black coffee and asked, "Where to next?"

"I'd like to see Lizzy's candle booth if that's okay?" Denise said.

"Oh boy! Yes, let's go check on my booth!" Lizzy said with a big smile.

Lizzy's booth was beautiful and smelled great before we even got to it. There were a few kids there making colored tapered candles, and her staff was already having to replenish the displays that she had out. Her candles were so festive! With big orange bows, or green ribbons. And the fall scents smelled scrumptious.

Among the small crowd at the candle booth, I spotted my

sister and her family. My five-year-old niece was making tapered candles. Her face was painted like a cat, and her little pink tongue stuck out the side of her mouth in concentration. It was adorable! When she hung her candles up to dry, I knelt down next to her.

"Summer! You look just like Clover!"

"Aunt Maddie!" She grabbed me around the neck with a huge hug. I laughed as we almost toppled over.

Sean gently pulled us apart. "Okay, Summer. You're gonna get face paint all over Aunt Maddie."

"That's okay by me," I said. "But I don't want Summer's cat face to get smeared."

Annabelle looked down at Summer with a smile and took her hand. "Let's swing by the face paint booth again and get your kitty face touched up." Looking back up at me, she said, "Good to see you, Sis."

I smiled back. "You, too. Glad you're giving yourself a much deserved break from work."

Hugs were exchanged, and Sean, Annabelle, and Summer went on their way, carrying their now-dry candles.

I turned back to the candle booth, eagerly rubbing my hands together. Even though I had a huge collection of Wicked Wicks candles already, I couldn't resist buying one with the scent of currants, blackberries, and patchouli. I smiled guiltily at Rick as he just shook his head.

"Like you couldn't already open your own store with all of the candles you own, Sis!"

"I know, I know!"

Booth-visiting duties done, we started walking toward the bonfire. Denise and I led the group, and Rick hung behind to walk with Lizzy. I swear, something was going on with those two! If I weren't so distracted by solving Matteo's murder - and now Brandon's - I might figure it out.

~

WE FINALLY CAME CLOSE TO THE BONFIRE. I STOPPED A BIT farther back than I had first intended as the fire was going strong, and so was the smoke. Everyone stopped with me.

"Hey guys, can we stand back here? I'm having a hard time with the smoke," I said.

"Sure, Maddie," Rick said.

I heard a familiar cough. Turning my head toward the sound, I saw Sharon and Steve. They each held one of the Yorkies in their arms. Sharon smiled at Steve as she pulled a long, silver strand of the dog's hair from Steve's sweater.

The hair on the back of my neck stood up.

Oh my god. The hair they found at the crime scenes was long and silver! It was *dog* hair!

Just then they both turned to look at me. Steve's eyes narrowed at me. His eyes showed both fear and anger. I knew I was in danger.

Fortunately, we were all in a public place, so for now I was safe. I moved closer to Rick, pretending that I didn't see or hear a thing, hoping desperately that I had imagined the look from Steve.

Steve whispered something to his wife and I saw Sharon's eyes move to me. She stared for a moment, then gave me a fake smile and wave. They nodded to each other, then moved away.

I must have visibly relaxed, because Rick asked, "What was that all about?" He looked at me with concern.

I stole a glance at Denise, who thankfully had missed the whole exchange. "I'll tell you later. Let's just try to enjoy the rest of the evening. But let's stick close together, okay?"

Chapter Nineteen

The next day, Jeremy, Rick, and Lizzy joined me at my place for a revised suspects discussion. Before everyone came over, I updated Matteo's detective board, to which I had added the photos of Steve and Sharon Christensen.

Now I was sitting on the couch next to Jeremy, my head on his shoulder, and Clover in my lap. "I'm telling you guys," I said, gently rubbing Clover's belly. "I'm sure it was Steve who was in the locker room the night I was attacked. The sound of his cough is branded into my brain. And then there's the dog hairs! I just know it's the same hairs that were found at Matteo's crime scene and on the racket. I think they were *Yorkie* hairs." I looked around the room. "And you should have seen the creepy smiles Steve and Sharon gave me." I shivered in remembrance.

Jeremy gave a low growl. "I can't believe I missed all of this!" His arm wrapped around me protectively. "It all makes sense though."

"That's crazy, Mads!" Lizzy said. "I'm so glad you were in a public place, and with all of us, when you realized this. And

I'm glad we had Rick with us." She looked over at Rick and gave him a grateful smile.

"I'm glad I was there, too," Rick said, smiling back. "So where are we then? What motive did he have?"

"Well," I said. "We know Steve was in the locker room. We also know Brandon was essentially stalking Denise. Maybe he was near the locker rooms when Steve killed Matteo and started blackmailing him," I suggested.

Brows crinkled around the room as everyone tried to digest this information.

"If Steve killed him," Jeremy asked, "then how did the racket end up in the *women's* locker room?"

"And why would Steve kill Matteo in the first place?" Lizzy asked.

"I don't have an answer for the racket," I said. "But maybe Steve found out that Matteo wasn't faithful to his daughter and killed him for it."

"Seems a pretty stiff penalty for being a ladies' man," Rick said.

"People have killed for less," Jeremy said grimly. We all nodded in agreement.

"Well, maybe it wasn't planned," I said. "Maybe it was a heat-of-the-moment kinda thing. A crime of passion. Anger can lead to all sorts of bad choices."

I looked back at the board. While I had exonerated Denise ever since I'd had that candle moment with her, she was still on the board, but more as a pawn stuck in the middle of all of these potential killers.

"Where does Sharon come in?" Lizzy asked. "I know you said she gave you a creepy look and was seemingly commiserating with her husband. Do you think she knows he's guilty of something?"

"I'm not really sure yet," I said. "I just wanted to leave her up there for now. Maybe she's the one who put the racket in the women's lockers to remove suspicion from her husband. There were a lot more women than men at the tournament. More potential suspects if and when the racket was found."

"That's an interesting thought," Jeremy said. "We should have DNA back soon from the racket. That will at least tell us the gender of the donors. And we can also use the DNA to get fingerprint exemplars from those people to compare to the prints on the racket. That is assuming that we can get names to go with the DNA."

"Seems like we're kinda in a holding pattern until that happens," Rick said.

"Yeah," I said. "We really need some solid evidence that backs up one of our theories."

Chapter Twenty

A few days later, Annabelle stood at the press room podium with some of her higher-ranking officers by her side. The press took their photos and stood ready to record what she had to say.

"Hello, and thank you for coming. My name is Annabelle Quinn Murphy, Chief of Police. We received the lab results for the DNA taken from the tennis racket found near the crime scene. We didn't find any matches to the DNA in CODIS - the Combined DNA Index System. However, based on the fact that this is a murder case, we were able to acquire a warrant to run the DNA against a commercially used genealogical database. This provided us with enough infor-mation to issue warrants for three members of our commu-nity as persons of interest. This will also allow us to get fingerprint exemplars from these persons for comparison to the fingerprints lifted from the tennis racket. While it was used in the commission of the crime, and is thus a key piece of evidence in this case, it was not the murder weapon. Cause of death was a broken neck from falling against a ceramic sink.

"We felt it important to protect the privacy of our citizens, and so decided against fingerprinting all attendees of the tournament. We strongly believe this was a crime of passion and opportunity, and believe the racket has provided us with the information we need to close the case.

"We're also making some progress on the murder of Brandon Lewis, and should have more information for you in a few days. We are executing warrants based on the evidence from the racket as we speak, and I hope to have one or more persons in custody soon. Our original suspect has been released, pending further inquiries. Thank you for your time. That's all we have for now, but I'll be taking questions."

Hands went up around the room.

"Yes, Randy?" Annabelle asked.

"I've heard that strands of long hairs were found at some of the crime scenes. Was the lab able to extract any DNA from those hairs?"

Annabelle shook her head. "No, those hairs were determined to be from a canine, so DNA was not something we collected." She looked around the room. "Yes, Maria?"

"Can you share with us why the suspect in Mr. Lewis's murder was released if there are no other suspects in the case?"

"I never said there were no other suspects in the case," Annabelle said. The room quieted at this news.

After taking a few more questions from the press, Annabelle and her officers moved into the hallway for some privacy while the press filed out the other doors.

I hovered nearby as inconspicuously as possible in order to eavesdrop on their conversation. Thankfully, being a younger sister often comes with the side benefit of being invisible to one's older sister.

Most of what they were saying was stuff I already knew

thanks to Jeremy and just hanging out at the station a lot. But then something Annabelle said caught my attention.

A light bulb went off in my head and I knew where to find the killer.

Or *killers*.

~

As I drove to their house, I thought about what I had overheard my sister tell her officers. The information was three-fold.

One, was that they had found two sets of DNA on the broken racket. These were from female donors that shared approximately fifty percent of their DNA. This meant that they were most likely mother and daughter.

Two, was that the DNA found on Clover's claws from when I was attacked outside of my town home was male and *also* shared approximately fifty percent of their DNA with one of the female donors from the racket. Most likely suggesting a father and daughter relationship.

Three, they confirmed that the silvery long hairs found at Matteo's crime scene and on the racket were from a Yorkshire Terrier! A detail Annabelle left out of her press conference, but told her officers in private.

There was only one family I could think of that had a mom, dad, and daughter that fit these three forensic clues *and* that were involved in the tennis community.

So after the press conference, I ran out to my car and drove straight to the Christensen's house.

Evening was approaching as I parked across the street from their house. I figured, if I could just get the chance to talk with Denise, I could use my new friendship with her to figure out the missing pieces as to who killed Matteo. I was so close! I was convinced that Matteo's killer was one of her parents. But which one? And why would they kill him? I was pretty sure that Denise could fill in the blanks, if I could just get her alone.

I got out of my car and crossed the street. I was about to knock on the front door when it flew open and I found myself staring into the face of a very angry Steve.

So far, things were not going as planned.

Before I could gather my thoughts and speak, he looked behind me to make sure no one was with me, then grabbed my arm and pulled me into the house.

He slammed the door shut and dragged me into their living room. He threw me toward a chair, then let go of my arm. I stumbled from the momentum, falling into the chair with enough impact to take my breath away.

I watched in shock as he grabbed some nearby rope and tied me to the chair. It seemed as though he was expecting me.

I was scared to death, but some part of my "just can't leave a mystery alone" brain said, *Ha! Guess I was on the right track!*

The scared part of my brain said, *Way to go, Mads. No one knows you're here.*

"Dad! What are you doing?!" Denise asked, having walked into the room just as he finished tying me to the chair.

"Keep quiet, Denise. I've got this handled."

"You've got *what* handled?" she asked, eyes wide.

"Denise, let us deal with this," said Sharon from somewhere behind me.

Oh, great. The whole gang was here.

THANKFULLY, MY BRAIN STARTED TO CATCH UP BECAUSE I HAD to think quickly. I needed a distraction, so I decided to share what I knew with them. Not as pleasant as a friendly conversation with Denise, but it would have to do.

Denise stood without moving in the corner of the room, looking shell-shocked. I had always suspected her innocence, and her behavior just served to reinforce that feeling. So I started with her.

"Denise," I said. "I always had the feeling that you were not involved with Coach Matteo's death. And although your racket, which naturally had your DNA and fingerprints on it, was used during the murder, you were taken off my list of suspects fairly early on." Actually, I didn't know for sure that her fingerprints were on the racket, but I figured if her DNA was, her prints probably were, too.

While I spoke, Steve glared at me, fists hanging by his side. Sharon paced the room restlessly.

"While you had the opportunity to kill Matteo, as did all of us who attended the tournament, I never felt you had a strong motive," I said. "You seemed to genuinely love him and were ignorant of his tendency to play around."

At this, Denise sunk to the floor crying. Apparently, she was still ignorant of this. Oops.

Denise's mom stopped pacing and sat down next to her, placing a comforting arm around her shoulders. Denise laid her head against her mom's chest.

"Steve, on the other hand..." I said.

His head swiveled around toward me at hearing his name. His eyes narrowed. "And what does little Miss Sherlock Holmes have to say about *me*," he asked.

Little Miss Sherlock, eh? Ha! I've heard worse!

"Based on the level of violence done to Matteo, for a long time we assumed that it had to have been a man that killed him."

"You'd be surprised at the damage a woman can do if

angry enough," he said. "Especially a well-trained woman. I was in the military police. I should know."

Wait, what? That threw me for a loop. How did I not know he had been an MP? I filed that info away in my brain for later. I was on a roll.

"Granted," I said. "But you had both motive and opportunity. As your wife and daughter were in the tournament, you had easy access to the men's locker room where Matteo was killed."

"So?" he asked. "For every four women there, there had to be at least one male."

"True again. But they didn't tamper with evidence and they didn't attack me twice!" I was getting angry again just thinking about it. "Actually, make that *three* times! The third, when I came here tonight!"

"I wasn't trying to 'attack' you in the locker room. You were just in my way. I warned you to leave us alone. But you just couldn't help yourself."

"Ha! So it *was* you that attacked me on my walk! You said, 'leave *us* alone,' not 'leave *me* alone.' And Clover got a nice little piece of your neck in her claws. I saw you scratching at it in my shop." At this, Steve scowled at me.

I knew it! And now I had proof! Proof that no one would ever know about, because I'm here by myself. Dang.

"Lastly," I said, "They found Yorkie hairs at Matteo's crime scene and on the bloody racket. This was the last clue that tied you to the crimes."

"And just what motive do you think I have?" Steve asked.

"Coach Matteo was seeing your daughter."

"So? Why would I kill him for that?"

Hmm. Good question. Think, Mads! Think! Ah! I got it...

"Because," I said, "you thought he was also seeing your *wife.*"

Oh, boy. That hit a nerve.

"What?!" Denise said, looking at her mom in disbelief. "You were sleeping with Matteo?" Denise started to cry again. This time, the tears were angry ones. She pulled away from her mom's arms.

Steve knelt in front of her, a sad look on his face. "No, sweetheart. Your mom was not cheating on me. On us. But it wasn't for lack of trying," he said. His anger had melted into grief. He moved to a chair and sat down with his face in his hands.

When he did, I breathed a little easier.

Sharon couldn't look her family in the eye. She stared down at the floor, quiet.

"Sharon," I said. "Like your husband, you also had motive and opportunity. Watching you at the tennis courts and at the tournament, it became clear to me that you wanted a relationship with Matteo. You were jealous of everyone he flirted with. Especially your daughter. That relationship was more serious than the other flings and this angered you. Add to that, she is you, only twenty years younger and prettier." At this, Sharon looked up at me and glared.

"It kinda made sense that your DNA would be on the racket. You did handle your daughter's tennis equipment from time to time. But your palm print told another story. It was high up on the handle of the racket. That meant you used the handle of that racket - but not for playing tennis. It was to beat Matteo. There are tool marks on his body to prove it. The stitching pattern where the strings attach to the frame of the racket is very distinctive. This pattern was on his body. You must have been very angry. How many times did you hit him after shoving him to the ground? Ten? Fifty? You must have-"

"Stop!" Sharon cried out. "I didn't *mean* to kill him! I swear it was an accident." Tears began to fall down her face as she told her story.

"It was after the tournament. We had won, and I was thrilled for Coach Matteo! This win would do great things for his career.

"I was also excited to see him alone. We had flirted a few times. I may be forty-two, but I *look* twenty-nine. And I could teach his young, twenty-something gorgeous body a few things if given the chance.

"I intentionally left Denise's tennis bag in the women's locker room so I had an excuse to go back after most of the players had left. I knew Matteo, being one of the coaches, would take a bit longer to leave the club.

"I was pretty sure I'd find him in the men's locker room, getting cleaned up for the party. He lived too far away to want to drive home and back.

"I entered the locker room still carrying Denise's tennis gear, so I set the bag down on the floor. I wanted to free my hands and body for a celebratory kiss.

"Matteo was standing in front of the bathroom mirrors washing his face and hands in the sink. He looked so handsome! His skin had a light sheen of sweat. I just wanted to touch it. His beautiful, dark olive, Italian skin.

"I reached out to him and spoke in a low, sultry whisper. 'Matteo...'

"He started to turn around in surprise. I thought for sure he had seen me behind him in the mirror. I guess he hadn't. Or at least he didn't think it was me. He was still smiling when he turned, saying, 'Denise! Back for more already?'

"We both looked at each other in shock.

"'Den-*ise?*' I was so stunned, I almost yelled my daughter's name.

"He asked me what I was doing there. He looked me up and down like he couldn't believe his eyes.

"I told him that I was there to help him celebrate.

"I walked toward him with a smile back on my face, and

said, 'Denise is just a child. A man like you needs a real woman.'

"But when I tried to drape my arms around his neck and give him a kiss, he actually made a sound of disgust and pushed me away! Disgust? For *me*?

"Anyway, I don't know what happened. I've never been rejected like that. Men adore me. How dare he push me away?

"The next thing I knew, he was on the bathroom's tile floor. There was blood on the sink. Blood on his head. Blood on the floor...

"I looked down at my hands and saw my daughter's racket in them. I was hitting him with it. Yelling at him.

"When I came to my senses, I panicked. I knew I couldn't take my daughter's racket back home with me. It was broken and covered in blood. So I shoved it into the tennis bag and just ran out of there with the bag. Not knowing what else to do, I went to the women's locker room to clean up and then tossed the racket on top of the lockers.

"I never meant to cause everyone so much pain," Sharon said. "My daughter..." She looked sadly at Denise who just stood staring in shock. "My sweet husband..." Steve sat on a chair, his face in his hands, shoulders shaking with grief.

"You." She looked at me, then hung her head in shame.

"Well," I said, "You could start your penance by maybe untying me?" I suggested gently.

"Oh, my god, yes. I'm so sorry!" She ran over and removed the ropes from my wrists and ankles. I stood up slowly and gingerly rubbed my raw skin.

I looked over at a shadowed hallway and gave a nod. To my extreme relief, about halfway through Sharon's confession I noticed that my sister had come in through a back door with her gun drawn. When she saw me tied up, her eyes went wide and she started toward me. An exclamation of surprise and concern was about to break from her lips.

As subtly as I could, I shook my head in warning at her.

She hadn't yet come into the room, where she would have seen the three people who were a party to this kidnapping.

Thankfully, she stopped. Years of sisterly silent communication paid off in spades. She was able to hear the rest of Sharon's confession.

Now, she came out of the shadows.

At the sight of the Chief of Police, Sharon started to cry heavily. This time, it was Denise's turn to comfort her mom.

"Nobody move," Annabelle said. "I have warrants for the arrest of Steve and Sharon Christensen."

Steve, who'd seemed like he was about to bolt - or maybe grab me as a hostage again - visibly deflated in defeat when he saw Annabelle's gun pointed at him.

Having decided he was the biggest threat at the moment, she cuffed him first. Then Sharon. By this time, backup had arrived and they took Sharon and Steve into custody.

Jeremy was with the backup and ran over to give me a bear hug. I could hardly breathe, but it sure was nice.

"Please don't ever do that again!" he pleaded into my shoulder, voice catching with emotion.

"I'm sorry I scared you," I said. I gently pulled away from him and turned to my sister. "Both of you."

But I couldn't promise never to do something like this again.

I just hoped they didn't notice.

LATER ON, BACK AT THE STATION, JEREMY TOOK THE ROPE AND other evidence of my kidnapping to the labs for processing.

I sat with Detective Dougan and Annabelle in her office. I

gave a quick thanks to the universe that we weren't back in that interrogation room. That place smelled of sweat and fear.

I asked the question that had been bothering me since Annabelle showed up at the Christensen's house.

"How did you know where I was?"

"Well, it wasn't thanks to you letting someone know what you were up to," said Detective Dougan with a frown. Still not my biggest fan, I see.

"I know, but I'd only planned to talk to Denise. Get her to fill in some blanks for me. I didn't expect to be abducted right off her front porch!"

"Fair enough," Annabelle said. "But next time, maybe just give me a heads-up first?"

I nodded with as much repentance as I could muster.

"And to answer your question, I knew you had sneaked into the press briefing and had followed us into the hallway. It was lucky that I was looking in your direction when I mentioned the DNA results. I didn't think you were close enough to hear us, but I could tell by the look on your face that not only could you hear us, but that you knew exactly what the results meant - that we had three samples of DNA which showed a familial relationship. So I followed you."

"Wow. Thank you, Sis. And I am sorry. Truly. I guess I didn't think it through all that well," I admitted. "I really didn't expect Steve to be so... angry and mean."

"Speaking of Steve, we also confirmed that he was the one who attacked you on your walk with Clover. His DNA was all over her claws. Be sure to give her a good ruffling and a cat treat from me for looking after you!"

I smiled. "You got it, Sis."

"Last but not least, at your suggestion, we looked into the financial records of Brandon," Annabelle said. "As he's dead, and the victim of a murder, it wasn't hard to get access to his accounts. You were right. He was blackmailing someone. And it wasn't Masayuki. It was Steve Christensen!"

"Oh, wow. I thought Steve was the one being blackmailed, but I had the wrong reason," I said. "What was he being blackmailed for?"

"Turns out, Brandon was stalking Denise when Sharon came out of the men's locker room carrying a bloody racket and looking freaked out from having killed Coach Matteo. He saw enough to scare Steve into paying."

"What made Steve finally decide to just kill Brandon instead of paying him?" I asked.

"Brandon wasn't the smartest cookie," Annabelle said. "He got greedy. Kept raising the blackmail amount until it wasn't manageable anymore."

"Wow. Well, it sounds like he got what was coming to him," I said. "By the way, if your people were keeping an eye on him for stalking Denise, why weren't you able to prevent his murder?"

Annabelle sighed. "Yes, we were watching him so that his stalking of Denise didn't escalate to her assault or murder. But we just didn't have the manpower to watch him all the time, so we had to assume that when he was at home, Denise was safe. What we didn't expect was for someone to murder *him*."

I nodded in agreement. "Makes sense. And please know that I wasn't implying that you were responsible for his death!" She smiled at me and I sighed in relief. "And poor Coach Masayuki! To be framed for something he didn't do."

"Yes, it was pretty clever of Steve. He drugged Masayuki, which allowed him to not only break into his house and steal one of his sushi knives, but also effectively ruin any chance at whatever alibi he might have had at the time of the murder."

"Aww. Coach Masayuki is such a nice guy. I'm glad he's been exonerated."

"Yes, all charges have been dropped," she said.

"That's great to hear. Thanks for letting me know," I said.

"Just one more thing," Annabelle said. "As it turns out, you have been chosen to receive the ten thousand dollar reward for the information that led to the arrests in Coach Matteo's murder. What do you want to do with it?"

Wow. I had totally forgotten about that! "Um, well, I'd like to donate it to a charity. Can we find out if the coach's parents have a favorite?"

Annabelle smiled at this. "Great idea, Sis. I'll find out."

Chapter Twenty-One

Saturday, October 25

Coach Masayuki and I ran into each other at the tennis club. He stopped me and asked for a quick word.

"Madeline, I wanted to thank you for the effort you put into clearing my name of murder. When I called out to you in desperation that day, I had no reason to hope you'd want to help me." Coach Masayuki looked down at his hands in shame. "I had not treated you well after Matteo's death. I thought you were just prying into my personal and professional life. You deserved better than that. Thank you for treating me better than I treated you."

I was stunned into silence for a moment at his heartfelt words of gratitude. "I'm just glad I could help," I said modestly. "It's nothing the police wouldn't have eventually figured out." And I truly believed that. For the most part. "I knew you weren't capable of killing Brandon. You're a good person, Coach."

"It's nice to know you still believe that about me. I'd like to offer you free tennis lessons for as long as you want them, as a way of thanking you."

"Oh, wow. That's very generous of you! But I don't know if that's being fair to you. I just dug around in some trash. Apparently, I can't help myself when there's a mystery to be solved." I gave a short laugh.

"And for that, I am grateful! And besides, you're an excellent tennis player," he said. "It would be an honor."

We made arrangements for the first tennis lesson, then went our separate ways.

～

LATER THAT NIGHT, IT WAS TIME TO CELEBRATE WITH AN extended family night dinner! This time, it was going to be a large crowd.

Lizzy's parents, Emma and Dan Mitchell, were coming in order to celebrate everything getting back to normal in Sycamore Cove. Everyone was eager to move past the two murders.

I also invited Jeremy to the dinner. I wanted him to meet my family. And the more, the merrier, my mom always said. We thrived on having multiple conversations at one time.

With Pops, Summer, and Annabelle's husband Sean in attendance, that made twelve of us, including myself. I would have even brought Clover, but she didn't get along very well with Mom's shih tzus.

We all arrived at around the same time and gathered in the kitchen while Mom finished up the final touches of the meal.

"Camille, are you sure there isn't anything I can do?" Emma Mitchell asked for the fifth time, hovering nearby.

My mom laughed. "I'm sure, Emma. Please, just enjoy your wine and your husband's company. I'm nearly done."

At the suggestion, Emma joined Dan who was having a conversation with my dad about woodworking.

"If we're going to continue to have this many folks over at one time," Dad said, "I'm gonna have to make us a larger dining room table!"

Rick, who was sitting at the kitchen island's bar said, "Agreed. But for tonight we added a folding table that will work. Us 'kids' can sit there. And by that, I mean me, you..." Rick looked at me when he said this, "as well as Lizzy, and Summer."

"Yay!" Summer said with a big smile. This got us all to laugh.

"What about me?" Pops asked, looking at Summer.

Summer rolled her eyes. "You're not a kid, Pops."

"Yeah, Pops!" Rick said with a wink.

"Dinner is served!" Mom called out over the noise of conversations and laughter. "Come fill your plate and find your place at the table." Mom's table decorations could grace the front of Home & Gardens magazine, and her name cards were all handmade and reflected that person's personality. Mine, for example, had a photo of Clover "holding" a tennis racket.

I held back a bit to let folks move ahead of me in the line for food. I also wanted to check on Jeremy, who had been rather quiet since he'd arrived.

I stood close to him, leaned over, and said in a quiet voice, "Did I scare you away? I know my family can be a lot to take in."

He looked at me wide-eyed, and said, "It's amazing. It's wonderful. And I love it." He gave me a big smile.

I gave him a smile back. "Then let's dig in!" I moved my wine to my left hand, grabbed his hand with my right, and pulled him forward to collect our dinner plates.

Mom had really outdone herself tonight. She'd made prime rib, roasted garlic vegetables, and mashed potatoes. Jeremy chuckled as I piled the food onto my plate. "What?" I asked. "I'm just getting my seconds now, so I don't have to get up again."

He nodded slowly and raised an eyebrow at me in understanding. "Ah. Clever girl." He followed suit, adding another generous scoop of potatoes to his own plate.

We made our way to the table. I laughed when I saw that Mom had put Jeremy at the "adult's" table, and me next to him, but at the kid's table.

Summer sat to my left, and Rick and Lizzy sat across from us on the other side of the kiddie table.

As usual, a handful of conversations sprang up at one time.

I eyed Rick as he leaned close to Lizzy, pretending to check out her food selection. Lizzy batted her eyes at him. Oh boy. How did I not see *that* coming?

Pops and Dad continued the conversation about the new dining room table that Dad was going to build. "If possible, I'd like to have it done by Christmas dinner," Dad was saying. "I'll design it with two or three leaves, allowing us to resize as needed." Pops nodded in agreement.

Emma and Dan were leaning into each other, holding hands. "I'm so glad that horrible business is over with," Emma said. Dan didn't reply, he only reached up and gently tucked a stray lock of hair behind her ear, then gave her a quick kiss, looking around to see if he'd been spotted. I winked at him when he caught my eye, and he actually blushed!

Summer kept trying to talk to her dad, even though Sean was on the other side of the larger table. Finally, Rick got up and switched places with Summer so she could be closer to her dad. That earned him an "Aww!" of admiration from Lizzy.

"That's right..." Sean was saying to Summer. He cleared his throat. "Everyone? I'd like your attention for a moment." The room got quiet. "Summer would like for you all to know that next year at this time, she will be in the first grade." Summer beamed with pride at this, while Annabelle groaned.

"Honey," Annabelle said, "let's not rush things, alright?" At Summer's pout, she added, "It will certainly be exciting, but let's enjoy kindergarten first."

"Yeah!" Rick added. "You've only just started. Give it a chance. There's finger painting, and paper mache, and learning your numbers..."

Summer didn't look convinced, so I changed the subject. "So where are we doing Thanksgiving next month?"

"I'm glad you brought that up!" Emma said. "I'd like to invite you all to our house. We have plenty of room and would love to host. We have so much to be thankful for, after all."

Yes, they did have plenty of room. The Mitchell home was more of a compound. They owned ten acres of rolling green hills, and had a stable that could board up to twelve horses. They also had a pasture complete with free roaming chickens (and a rooster, of course), a few pigs, and one noisy goat. The home itself was a sprawling ranch style and had to be close to eight thousand square feet, complete with a bocce ball court, an underground wine cellar, and huge library, of which I was particularly jealous.

Everyone immediately agreed and started to make plans for who would bring what part of the meal, the football game (to be watched in the media room), and what board games we would play.

I leaned back in my chair, sipped my wine contentedly, and marveled at how lucky I was to have such wonderful people in my life.

Chapter Twenty-Two

Sunday, October 26

It was another sunny day in Sycamore Cove, California, and Denise, Lizzy, and I were enjoying a horseback ride down a local trail designed just for this type of thing. I love our small town!

As we meandered along the winding, shady bridle path, we chatted amiably about various things: love, work, and so on.

For most of the ride, I'd been trying to think of a non-invasive (and non-offensive!) way of asking Denise how she was doing. I mean, her parents were now both in jail! How does anyone deal with that? But I could think of no good segue, so I just asked with love in my heart.

"Denise... I've been worried about you since this whole thing with your parents. Particularly because I feel somewhat responsible for, you know, catching them..." I trailed off weakly.

"Whoa!" Denise said, pulling on her horse's reigns to bring the horse to a stop. Denise looked upset, so I also stopped, with Lizzy stopping next to us. I braced for the worst.

"Don't you *dare* blame yourself for my parents' bad choices, Mads!" she said, her voice heated. Then she closed her eyes and sighed heavily. Her face fell. Denise's horse neighed gently in seeming response to her sudden sadness.

Opening her eyes again, I saw that they were bright with unfallen tears. "Thank you for being my friend. Both of you," she said, her gaze taking in Lizzy, too. "Thankfully, I'm an adult and have no need to live with my parents. Not legally anyway. However, I do feel a bit overwhelmed by it all, so my aunt is coming to stay with me for a while."

"Oh! That's great news," I said. "I'm so relieved that you won't be alone."

"Agreed," Lizzy said. "And if you ever need company, we're available!"

We all started moving down the trail again.

"Well, I'd be up for doing this at least once a month!" Denise said with a smile.

"Deal!" Lizzy and I said at the same time. We all laughed.

Yep. Things were looking up.

~ THE END ~

❧

THANK YOU FOR READING THIS BOOK! IF YOU ENJOYED IT, I would greatly appreciate a review (adding a photo of the book is even better!).

❧

IF YOU'D LIKE TO STAY INFORMED ABOUT THE MADELINE Quinn Mystery world (such as when Book 2 is coming out, in-person events, or special offers), please sign up for our newsletter!

www.MoniqueLStover.com

About the Author

Monique L. Stover has always had a nose for mysteries—first as an avid young reader of Nancy Drew and Sherlock Holmes, now as a cozy mystery author. A native of sunny Southern California, she earned her master's degree in Anthropology and certification in Forensic Identification before putting her investigative skills to work at the Ventura County Crime Lab. These days, she uses that same attention to detail (and love of a good puzzle) to craft her *Madeline Quinn Mystery* series, where a curious amateur sleuth and her tuxedo cat, Lucky Clover, find trouble lurking behind every tennis ball and tidepool.

Monique's thrillers, written under *M. L. Stover*, prove she's equally at home in the shadows—but she's happiest writing stories where the murder is tidy, the motives are tangled, and the cats always have the last word.

When she's not plotting fictional crimes, Monique can be found at book club, on the tennis court, or crunching numbers as a financial analyst. She shares her Southern California home with her music producer husband, and three cats—Enzo, Porsche, and Bianka—one of whom insists on her own literary alter ego.

Connect with Monique L. Stover

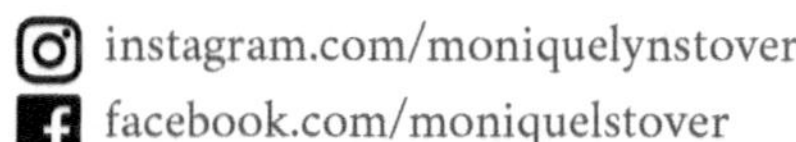

instagram.com/moniquelynstover

facebook.com/moniquelstover

Also by Monique (writing as M. L. Stover):

Provectus: Survival of the Fittest

Calm Before the Storm: A Provectus Network Novella

www.ingramcontent.com/pod-product-compliance
Lightning Source LLC
Chambersburg PA
CBHW030924060726
47591CB00005B/1653